Caught in the Crosshairs

Danger in Destiny
Book 4

Melanie D. Snitker

DALLIONE MEDIA, LLC

Caught in the Crosshairs
Danger in Destiny: Book 4
By Melanie D. Snitker

All rights reserved
© 2024 Melanie D. Snitker

Dallionz Media, LLC
P.O. Box 5283
Abilene, TX 79608

Cover Art: Dallionz Media, LLC

Melanie D. Snitker
melanie@melaniedsnitker.com
www.melaniedsnitker.com

This is a work of fiction. Names, characters, businesses, places, events, and incidents either are the products of the author's imagination or used in a fictitious manner. Any resemblance to actual persons, living or dead, or actual events is purely coincidental.

You are my hiding place;
You will protect me from trouble
and surround me with songs of deliverance.
Psalm 32:7

Chapter One

A glance at her watch gave Erica Keyes a renewed sense of urgency. "Peter, come on, honey! We're going to be late!"

"I'm trying!" Her eight-year-old's words were muffled as he chewed. He shoved his lunch box inside his favorite backpack, pulled it on over his right shoulder, and then stuffed the last bite of a cinnamon roll in his mouth.

Erica tossed him a disapproving look. She thought about reminding him not to eat and talk at the same time, but he already knew. Besides, they were pushing it if they were going to get Peter dropped off at school on time.

Why were Mondays always like this?

She slung her purse over one shoulder. "All right, kiddo. Let's go."

They left the kitchen of Tranquil Bed & Breakfast, where she was owner and manager, and made their way toward the main room. Erica had owned the business for some years now, and she and Peter lived there as well. It made getting to work easy, at least.

She looked up as her morning manager, Bethany Massy, entered.

"Hey, Erica. Hi, Peter. Sorry, I'm running a little late today."

"Please, don't worry about it. I think it's the theme for the day." Erica chuckled. "How are you doing?"

The younger woman smiled brightly. It matched the mood of her vibrant purple hair perfectly. "I'm doing great. How about you?" She stored her bag in the drawer behind the front counter and locked it.

"Not bad. I could have used more sleep. Then again, isn't that always the case?"

"Definitely," Bethany affirmed. "I was up way too late last night studying statistics. We've barely started the class, and I'm already feeling overwhelmed."

"Hopefully that'll get better as the class continues."

"I sure hope so." She waved at Peter. "Have a good day at school."

He grinned. "I will!"

Erica put a hand against her son's backpack and directed him toward the front door. "I have a couple of errands to run, but I won't be long," she said to Bethany over her shoulder.

"Not a problem. See you in a while." With a wave, Bethany turned her attention to tidying up the counter.

Erica had hired Bethany as a part-time manager about six months back, finally realizing that she needed more help. The younger woman had been a godsend. She managed everything from seven until eleven in the morning and then again from three until seven in the afternoon. That allowed Erica the freedom to take Peter to school and pick him up afterward. It also meant she could get errands done, help out at the Nazarene church when needed, even meet her family for dinner.

Near the front door, Erica bent down to lift a large cardboard box. It wasn't nearly as heavy as it looked, but the dimensions and clothing packed inside made it awkward to carry.

The church was caring for a family who had just lost their home in a fire. Erica had a room upstairs in the B&B dedicated to donated clothing that was offered to anyone in need. She'd been up late last night gathering a variety of clothes for the couple and their young daughter, who were staying with family in town. She'd drop the box off at the church after taking Peter to school and maybe even swing by and get a fancy coffee before coming back to work. She could sure use the pick-me-up today.

It was the middle of September, which wasn't usually a busy time of the year for the B&B. Especially since school started up again last month. There were currently two guests with no reservations in the books for the next two weeks.

One of the guests was a businessman by the name of Sebastian Rumford. He was in town for a conference on customer service.

The other was a man named Cole Shepherd who came in on Saturday. Now he was an interesting guy. He might have been only two inches taller than her, but he was built like a truck. With broad shoulders, thick biceps, and a wide stance, he came off as a guy you wouldn't want to meet in a dark alley.

And yet, he'd been nothing but friendly and polite.

He said he was looking at commercial properties and would be around for a few days, but she knew little else about him.

Speaking of the man...

Cole came downstairs, his hands buried in the pockets of his jeans. As soon as he spotted Erica, he jogged forward and lifted the box of clothing right out of her arms. "Here, let me get that for you. Good morning, you two."

"Thank you," Erica held the front door open so he could carry the box outside. "And good morning."

"Hey, Mr. Shepherd," Peter said with a wave.

"You off to school?"

"Yes, sir."

"Awesome." Cole glanced up at the sky. "Looks like it's going to be a beautiful day." He waited for Erica to open the back of her blue Sentra and loaded the box for her.

She shut the trunk and gave him a smile. "I appreciate it."

"Not a problem. I'm heading into town myself. I've got an appointment with a realtor first thing." He took his keys out of his pocket. "You guys be careful and have a good day."

"Thanks. Good luck with your appointment." Erica said.

Peter waved goodbye, and Cole gave them a friendly nod as he climbed into his white pickup truck. Once behind the wheel, he reached for some paperwork in the passenger seat and started to rummage through it.

They loaded up in the Sentra, and Erica watched in the rearview mirror to make sure Peter got buckled in. It was already stuffy inside, and it was easy to tell that it was going to get hot today. Just because it was September, it did not mean summer weather was over completely. Not in Destiny, Texas, anyway.

She switched the air conditioner on low and drove around the circular drive before pulling onto the street.

They lived on the edge of town, which meant it took

about fifteen minutes to drive to Peter's school. It was also why she refused to send him by bus. By the time the bus meandered its way around to gather kids, he would be on it for over an hour.

It might take fifteen minutes, but it was a peaceful drive. The country road had houses on one side with pastures and trees on the other. It was as close to living in the country as Erica could get without actually doing so.

Peter was chatting away in the back seat, telling her about PE the Friday before and how his best friend, Shane, had intentionally tackled one of the other boys too hard. "But George wouldn't stop teasing one of the new kids. He was being mean. And no one noticed since everyone was tackling each other anyway."

She loved that Peter and his friend were the type of kids who welcomed newcomers, stood up for those who were being bullied, and were generally great kids. Not only did they go to school together, but they were part of the same youth group at church.

"Hopefully George got the hint and will leave the new kid alone."

"I hope so. We're going to invite him to sit with us at lunch. The new kid, I mean. I think his name was Axel. Axe." Peter made a face. "Something like that. I'll have to ask him again."

Erica pulled up to a stop sign and turned right onto the three-mile stretch with nothing but pastures on either side.

Peter leaned forward in his seat. "Can you play some DC Talk?"

She looked at her son in the rearview mirror and gave him a nod. "You bet." She was more than happy that Peter tended to like the same music she did. In moments, he was belting out the words to "Jesus Freak."

She'd lived in Destiny her whole life and was glad that she'd never had to move away. She was even more thankful that her parents, brother, and sister-in-law lived here, too. They were all a huge help since she was raising Peter on her own. Her dad and brother were the father figures in Peter's life since his own father had never been a part of it. In November, Peter would even have a little cousin. Erica smiled at the thought of holding her baby nephew once he made his grand entrance into the world.

The sound of an engine drew her attention to the rearview mirror. A large, black vehicle was closing in fast. It wasn't unusual for people to take the narrow country road at unsafe speeds. An accident was reported along this stretch at least once a month.

Erica muttered under her breath and slowly eased partly onto the shoulder to allow them plenty of room to pass.

Instead of roaring past her like she'd expected, the SUV matched her speed for a few moments. She glanced over and noticed a man in the passenger seat staring straight at her. It was long enough to note his narrow face, large nose, and a baseball cap with a logo she didn't recognize.

Suddenly, the black SUV jerked to the right, hitting them with a sickening crunch and a squeal of metal against metal.

She gripped the steering wheel and struggled to keep her vehicle from veering off the road and into the ditch and embankment beyond. A dozen thoughts screamed through her head.

What was happening? Who was that man? Who was driving? Why were they hitting her car?

She looked in the rearview mirror just long enough to register the frightened look on her son's face.

"Peter. I need you to hang on, honey. We're going to be okay."

They had to be.

"Father," she whispered fervently as the SUV slowed down in front of them as though waiting for them to catch up, "please keep us safe."

There was less than a mile to go until they reached a more populated road.

If they truly were trying to run her off the road, they would have to try again before they reached the edge of town and risked getting caught.

The realization struck her as though someone had poured a bucket of ice water down the back of her shirt.

Their vehicles were nearly side-by-side when Erica pressed the gas pedal, shooting past the SUV.

But her little car was no match for them, and there was nowhere for her to go.

The SUV rammed into her car again, then took off with a roar.

With a prayer trapped in her throat, Erica's fingers tightened around the steering wheel as they careened off the road, hit the ditch hard, and went airborne until they were stopped by a tree.

Every muscle and bone in her body was violently shaken as the car came to an abrupt stop.

Steam rose from the hood with a hiss. The airbags had deployed, filling the car with a horrible smell that burned her lungs. The car had struck the tree on the front passenger side. The dashboard was practically pushed into the seat.

Anyone sitting there would have been killed instantly. Bile fought its way up her throat. She swallowed hard.

"Peter! Peter!" Erica tried to turn in her seat to see if her son was okay.

Peter looked stunned. He pressed his right hand to the side of his face and pulled it back. When he saw the blood, his eyes widened. "Mom?"

"Thank you, God," she said in a whisper as she removed her seatbelt. Frantic, she looked in the direction of the road. There was no sign that the SUV had doubled back, but between the angle of the embankment and the trees, it was impossible to see the road itself from her position. She wasn't about to risk waiting in the car like sitting ducks, especially since her car wasn't going anywhere soon.

Erica tried to find her cell phone, which had been in the cup holder in the console, but it was gone. She moved her foot around the floor but couldn't find it.

She knew this area like the back of her hand. The Patton's home was on the other side of this tree line. If they could reach it, she could call for help.

With some effort, she clambered out of the car and ran around to the other side. She had to push past thick branches to reach Peter's door and force it open.

Erica reached across to release his seatbelt and helped him out. She grabbed his backpack off the floorboard and handed it to him, then snatched several tissues from the box on the floor. She pressed them against the wound on his head, causing him to flinch. "Are you okay?"

The blood continued to trickle from the small cut on his forehead. It might need a stitch or two, but it wasn't too serious. At least she prayed it wasn't.

Peter's face paled as he looked at his hands and then shifted his weight. "I think so."

She pressed a kiss to the top of his head and directed his hand to hold the tissues. "Keep those right there. Okay?"

Peter nodded and hefted his backpack onto one shoulder.

The sudden sound of a vehicle door slamming made him jump and sent Erica's heart into overdrive.

He looked up at her, his eyes wide. "Did they come back?"

"I don't know." But she wasn't about to wait around and find out.

Chapter Two

Outside the B&B, Cole found the information for the realtor he was supposed to connect with in a couple of hours and set it on the passenger seat. He figured he'd go into town, look around a little, and then meet with Tanya Lewis at the first address they were supposed to see.

He pulled his white pickup onto the country road that led into town. A ways ahead, he could see Erica's little blue car as it traveled in the same direction. Thinking about his hostess brought a smile to his face.

When he first checked in on Saturday, she'd been there to welcome him. Between her striking blue eyes and sweet smile, he'd been instantly captivated. Something that didn't happen very often. She appeared to be a single mom. At least she didn't wear a wedding band, and a husband never made an appearance.

Her son, Peter, was a great kid. He was friendly and talkative, and helped his mother. He was also a bit mischievous, which, if you asked Cole, was an important ingredient in any curious young boy's life.

But it was watching the way Erica interacted with her son that had pulled at Cole's heartstrings. She was firm with Peter yet so incredibly patient and loving.

The polar opposite of Cole's own mother, or at least from what he could remember of her after all these years.

What would his life have been like if his mother had shown even a fraction of the love and support Erica showed her son?

It was better not to dwell on the what-ifs in life. They led down a serious rabbit hole that could be incredibly difficult to dig out of again.

He reached for the rest of a bear claw that he'd tossed into the cup holder when he first jumped in and finished it in two bites. Even the packaged breakfast items Erica's business provided during the work week were better than what he'd gotten at most hotels. Sunday morning? It'd been like eating a home-cooked meal and rivaled most restaurants. He could still taste the ham, eggs, and hashbrowns. It was almost enough to make him want to stay through this coming weekend.

Up ahead, Erica's car stopped and turned onto another road. When he got to the intersection, he checked for traffic and did the same thing.

Not thirty seconds later, a black SUV with tinted windows pulled off a side road behind her. Cole might not have thought much of it, but there was something about the way the SUV seemed to swerve in the lane that had him taking notice.

And then they sped up, well over seventy miles per hour—way too fast for this little road.

Erica's car pulled over onto the shoulder ahead. He hoped they wouldn't clip her when they passed.

Except they never did. Instead, they seemed to hover beside her car before swerving and ramming right into her.

Cole swallowed a curse, stomped on the gas pedal, and wished there wasn't as much distance between himself and Erica.

"Come on. Come on!" Cole chanted as his truck ate away at the distance between them.

To Erica's credit, she kept her car on the road.

Unfortunately, the SUV wasn't giving up. With another roar, it hit the rear of her car, sending the smaller vehicle off the road, into the ditch, and out of sight.

The SUV didn't come out unscathed. The collision forced it into the opposite lane. Thankfully, there was no oncoming traffic.

Cole didn't know if the occupants of the SUV had accomplished their goal, given up, or if they'd seen Cole's vehicle and decided to get out of there while they could. Either way, they were speeding on down the road before he could make out the license plate.

He pulled off the road near the tree line, got out of his truck, and was comforted by the feel of his handgun against his lower back. If the driver of the SUV changed his mind and came back, Cole would be ready.

After following the tire tracks to the ditch, his eyes went to Erica's car a short way down the embankment. It'd hit a tree, and the damage to the front was significant.

He kept his breathing steady as he crossed the ditch.

To his relief, Erica was on her feet on the other side of the car, and Peter was standing beside her. They were hand-in-hand and heading for the trees. She threw a look over her shoulder, startled when she saw him, and hesitated.

"Erica. It's Cole Shepherd from the B&B." He held a

hand up hoping to stop her. "I saw what happened, and I'm here to help."

She sagged with relief and slipped an arm around her son's shoulders. They waited for him to reach their position. Erica pointed in the direction of the road. "If they come back..."

Cole withdrew his phone and dialed 9-1-1 before putting it to one ear. "They took off," he told her as he waited for an operator to pick up the call.

Erica didn't look convinced. He put a steadying hand on her shoulder as a woman's voice came over the line.

"9-1-1. What is your emergency?"

As he relayed what happened, Cole visually inspected both Erica and Peter. "We've got some minor injuries, but one is a head wound."

"We'll be sending help your way, including an ambulance." There were some tapping noises in the background before the operator spoke again. "They are on the way, sir. If you would stay on the line with me until they get there, I'd appreciate it. Are both people who were in the accident able to stand on their own?"

"Yes. They're both standing." Cole looked at their car and swallowed a lump in his throat. It could have easily gone a different way. If the car had rotated before hitting that tree... He squeezed Erica's shoulder and noted that the sleeve of her blue T-shirt had a bloodstain that was slowly expanding. "It looks like we've got a shoulder wound too."

Erica looked at him in surprise. With all the adrenaline coursing through her veins, she probably couldn't even feel it.

Cole took a handkerchief from his pocket and pressed it against the back of her upper arm through the shirt. She flinched, and he gently rubbed his thumb across her bare skin.

Sirens pierced the air, distant at first, and then louder.

"Yes, I can hear them. I'm going to hang up. Thank you for your help."

Cole pocketed his phone. A minute later, he waved two police officers over as well as an EMT.

The female officer's eyes widened. "Erica?" She hurried forward. "Are you and Peter okay?"

"Jenny! I'm so glad you're here." Erica accepted a hug from the other woman. "I think so. Someone ran us off the road." She motioned toward her car where steam was still rising from the engine. "Peter has a cut on his head. I think it's superficial, but I'd like him to be checked out just in case."

"Absolutely. Hey, Curtis, over here." Officer Durant, according to the name badge on her uniform, directed Peter to sit on a fallen log. The EMT knelt beside him under Erica's watchful gaze.

The other officer, Baker, approached Cole. "Were you able to get a license plate number off the other vehicle?" His gaze flicked to Erica. "I'm glad you're okay, Erica."

She gave him a tight smile. "Thanks, Clint. I never could see the license plate in my rearview mirror. It was too close..."

"And both of their vehicles were too far ahead for me to make out the license plate." Cole wished he'd been able to report differently. "It was a black Chevy Tahoe. A '22 or '23. Tinted windows all the way around as best I could tell."

"Nice. That's helpful." Baker wrote that down. "I'm going to get a BOLO issued right now for a vehicle with that description and considerable damage to the body. See if we can track it down." He stepped away from them and called into dispatch.

"We should be able to get a sample of the paint too." Durant walked around Erica's car and whistled. "You and Peter are lucky you weren't hurt worse."

"I know." Erica's voice sounded tired. "God was watching out for us." She glanced at Cole. "And sent help."

Cole's stomach clenched. He was a Christian, but it'd been a long while since he'd shared much of his life with God. He sent up a silent prayer of thanks and wondered if God was ever surprised when one of His children made contact after so long.

The EMT, Curtis, stood and gave Erica a smile. "I don't think Peter has a concussion, but he could use a couple of stitches. Nothing major, though. He might have a small scar." He held his finger and thumb a quarter of an inch apart. "One of those cool scars the girls will love," he told Peter.

"Ewww." The look of disgust on the boy's face gave everyone a good chuckle.

Cole had yet to release the pressure he'd been holding against Erica's shoulder. He gently turned her so that Curtis could easily reach the injury.

Curtis gave a nod, and Cole took several steps back so he could have a look. Though it made zero sense, his hand felt cold and empty now that he was no longer touching Erica.

The EMT slowly rolled Erica's sleeve up until it was bunched on top of her shoulder. He used some gauze to swipe away the blood to get a better view. "It looks like a puncture wound." He focused on her face. "Do you remember hitting anything during the accident?"

Erica shook her head. She looked at the car and then the

tree it had crashed into. "I had to push branches away to get to Peter's door."

"That makes sense. It looks like there's some debris in the wound. We'd better clean it up and put in a stitch or two to keep it closed." Her arm was still bleeding, so he placed a fresh piece of gauze and wrapped it. "I can take you both to the hospital."

Erica didn't seem to like that idea. "If I could find my phone, I could call someone. I don't know what happened to it."

Cole took his own phone out. "What's your number?" He punched it in as she told him. Immediately, the sound of her phone ringing came from the car. He opened the driver's side door and stooped to pull it out from under the seat. With a triumphant smile, he ended the call and handed the phone to her.

"Thank you."

"You're welcome. Now, why don't you call whoever you need to and let them know what happened. I'll drive you both to the hospital."

If there was one thing about Destiny, Texas, it sure did step up to help its own. Once Cole got Erica and Peter to the hospital and the word got out, it was like things took on a life of their own.

By the time they all got back to the B&B, several people from Erica's church had brought food for the next two days. Erica's car had been towed away, and a rental car was supposed to be delivered by late afternoon.

Cole also had the opportunity to meet her brother and sister-in-law, Bryce and Megan. Bryce couldn't stay long because he was on duty at the fire department, but he still wanted to make sure his sister was doing okay. Megan worked as a nurse at the hospital, but today was her day off, so she hadn't been there when Erica and Peter came in. Cole also learned that Bryce and Megan were having their first baby—a boy—in November.

A spouse. Kids. Cole had never really seen that in his future. His own childhood had been a mess. The thought of being responsible for making sure that didn't happen with his own child was more than overwhelming.

And yet, watching the loving way in which Bryce and Megan looked at each other, he couldn't help but wonder what it would be like to love—and be loved by—someone so much.

His gaze shifted to Erica. They'd cleaned and patched up her wound. As soon as they got back to the B&B, she traded her ruined T-shirt for a purple blouse. Her brother kept her laughing, and the sound brought a smile to Cole's face as well.

Peter was doing okay. He had a small bandage on his head, and he seemed to be in good spirits. Currently, he was sitting on the couch in the living area, his backpack open and spilling over onto the cushion beside him. Erica kept him home from school, which was a good call.

Cole walked over to Peter and pointed to the backpack. He'd noticed it that morning. The whole front was covered with a variety of patches. "That's one of the coolest bags I've ever seen," he said.

Peter looked up and smiled. "Thanks! I have fifteen patches now," he said proudly.

"Where did you get them all?" Cole recognized several from state parks, and there were some character patches from TV shows or cartoons. There was one that said, "Best Nephew Ever" in bold writing.

Peter shrugged. "I started collecting them when we went on vacation last year. Once people knew I liked patches, they kept giving me new ones. One day, the whole bag will be covered!"

"I think that's a great hobby."

Peter seemed pleased and went back to reading his book.

Eventually, Bryce had to go back to the station. Megan offered to stay, but Erica insisted she was fine. Megan finally agreed to go home and get a nap, but only if Erica promised to keep them updated.

So far, there wasn't much in the way of news. The police hadn't found the SUV, and there was no reason anyone could think of as to why someone would have run her off the road in the first place.

Cole could see that they had a large support system. Even still, he hung around in the main part of the B&B where he could be a part of what was going on. He'd already called the realtor to reschedule for tomorrow with his apologies. That left him doing some property research of his own from the comfort of his laptop.

"Mom? Can I go play video games?" Peter looked up at his mother hopefully.

Erica placed a hand on his head and gently ruffled his hair. "Of course you can. Are you sure you don't need some Tylenol?"

The boy shook his head vigorously as though trying to prove he wasn't in any pain. "No, thank you."

"You were very brave. I'm proud of you." She gave him a kiss on the cheek. "Go on and play your video games."

"Yay!" He grabbed his backpack, tore out of the room, and bounded up the stairs.

Erica straightened a few things at the front counter and then made her way over to the living room. She took the recliner across the coffee table from the couch where Cole was sitting. She groaned as she leaned into the cushy back.

"What a long day. And it's not even two yet." She stifled a yawn.

"It's been grueling, for sure." He studied her and the way she'd allowed her eyes to close, her long lashes resting against her cheeks. When they opened again, she focused on his face as though she'd been able to tell he was staring.

"Thank you for stopping to help us. I'm glad you were right behind me."

"I am, too." Cole had gone through the whole scenario over and over. If he hadn't been there, would the driver of the SUV have left the scene like he did today? How far would Erica and Peter have had to walk to get help? "I'm just relieved that you guys are okay."

Erica put a hand on her shoulder and rubbed it gingerly. "So am I. I've heard of people just snapping in a fit of road rage. But this didn't make sense. I know I didn't cut them off or pass them too closely. I don't understand what set them off."

"And there's a good chance we may never know." Cole closed his laptop and set it aside. "I'm just sorry to hear that your car is likely totaled."

"Same." Erica sighed with a shrug. "But on a good note, at least having a rental is kind of like taking an extended test drive since I'll be in the market for a new car."

"That's a good way to look at it." He shot her an encouraging smile. "You handled the whole ordeal well, Erica. I saw the way you tried to stay on the road. You made them work for it."

"Thank you." She chuckled. "I'll have to figure out how to word that on my resume." The amusement on her face faded to concern. "I'm sorry that my whole mess made you miss the appointment with your realtor."

"It's not a big deal." He waved away her concern. "We rescheduled it for tomorrow morning. She found another property to show me anyway, so it worked out nicely."

The front door opened, and Officer Durant from earlier came inside.

Erica stood. "Any luck finding the SUV?"

"I wish I had better news." Officer Durant gave her a sympathetic look. "Unfortunately, you know how it is in this area. With a vehicle like that, they could've cut through a field or gone down any number of county roads. There's no telling where they went. And after running you off the road and knowing that Mr. Shepherd here saw the whole thing, if they were smart, they'd be halfway across Texas by now."

Erica motioned for the officer to join them, and the ladies sat down.

Officer Durant smiled again. "I did want to let you know that we filed the report, and we have a BOLO out on the SUV just in case it shows up. I also got that box of clothing over to the church for you."

"Thank you so much, Jenny."

"I wish there was more I could do to help." Officer Durant turned her attention to Cole. "It's a good thing you were there. How long are you in Destiny for?"

"Probably through the end of the week." Truthfully, he didn't need that long to look at properties. But he'd been struggling with whether to stay on and work for the business. It wasn't an easy decision, especially when family was involved. Some time away to think was exactly what he needed. There was an added benefit of making sure Erica and her son were okay before he left.

"Well, we're real glad you're here." Officer Durant gave him a nod of respect.

Erica seemed thoughtful as she stared out the large window at the front of the B&B. She gasped and leaned forward. "I can't believe I completely forgot!"

Cole rested his elbows on his knees. "What is it?"

"There were two guys in the SUV."

Officer Durant's eyebrows rose. "You're sure?"

"Without a doubt. The passenger window was rolled down, and the guy in that seat looked right at me." She visibly shivered, and Cole had to resist the urge to reach across the coffee table and touch her arm. "He wasn't memorable. I mean, it's not like he had this big scar on his face or anything. He was fairly thin with a long nose and a baseball cap."

The officer wrote that down in a notebook that she'd taken out of her pocket. "And you never saw the driver?"

"No." Erica frowned. "What are the odds that these guys might come looking for me since I saw one of their faces?" Her eyes were all serious as she looked from Cole to Durant.

"I think they're much more likely to hightail it out of here so that they don't get caught," the officer reassured her.

Cole agreed that was the most likely scenario, but that meant the men who essentially tried to kill Erica and Peter were still out there somewhere.

Chapter Three

Early Monday evening, Cole headed upstairs to his room at the B&B. The space was perfect for what he needed, with a large queen-sized bed, a couch along one wall, a small table and chairs in a corner, and a large cabinet that supported a TV. There was even a microwave on a small stand beside it.

A large blue and green rug on the floor matched the curtains, bringing color to the room. Had Erica decorated it herself?

Cole reached into a side pocket of his rolling suitcase and pulled out a caramel Twix. He never left home without a small stash of them. Instead of opening it right away, he set it on the table for later.

After eating a hearty dinner of barbecue provided by someone at Erica's church, Cole was still pretty full. He couldn't remember ever having brisket or jalapeno creamed corn that good.

He claimed a spot on the couch and took out his phone to call his half-brother. Malcolm, or Mac as everyone called him, would be waiting for an update on the property search.

Cole ignored the guilt that stabbed at him like a sliver buried deep in his skin. While the Durham clan was looking to relocate the private security company that had been in the family for years, Cole was seriously considering bowing out. It wasn't that he didn't like working in the field —it was more that he was a loner. Always had been.

Mac was the only member of the Durham family who Cole had any blood relation to. He appreciated all that the large family had done for him, but maybe it was time to step out on his own. He had to talk to Mac about it. Soon.

For now, there was something else he wanted to discuss.

The phone rang three times before Mac's deep voice came over the line. "Hey, man. I was just wondering how everything went today. Lay it on me. Any luck?"

Cole rotated to lounge on the couch, his head resting on one arm and his shoes on the other. "Not yet. I was supposed to meet with a realtor first thing this morning, but I had to reschedule for tomorrow. Today hasn't gone according to plan." He relayed the series of events, concluding with what little information the police had been able to gather.

Mac let out a long whistle. "It's a good thing you were there. You don't think it's random, do you?"

"Truthfully? I don't know. An SUV like that coming off a side road and gunning right for Erica's car? She said the guy in the passenger seat looked right at her. It doesn't feel like road rage to me."

"What do you need?"

"The local police are trying to track the vehicle down, but I don't think they're going to have much luck. If Asher has time, see what he can find on Erica Keyes. She owns Tranquil Bed & Breakfast, has an eight-year-old son named Peter, and it looks like she's single. I'm pretty sure she's lived in Destiny for a while." Cole hated doing a background search without her permission. It felt dishonest. At the same time, maybe there was something related to her or even the B&B that had painted a target on her today.

"Got it. I'll have him check into her, and I'll get back to you when we know anything."

"I appreciate it. How's your dad doing?"

Gregory Durham had founded Durham Security, but he acted more as the president of the company, making the big decisions but allowing Mac to take care of the day-to-day operations. Greg was larger than life, fiercely loyal, and had taken Cole in when he was just an angry thirteen-year-old.

For the last few months, Greg had been fighting cancer. Things were looking good, and the doctors were optimistic that he would make a full recovery. Still, as tough as Greg liked to pretend he still was, it was clear the radiation treatment was taking a toll.

Mac grunted. "You know Dad. Stubborn. Mom's keeping him in line. He's doing okay."

The illness was a big reason why Greg had decided to move Durham Security from just outside San Antonio to Destiny. That's where he had grown up, and he looked forward to living in a friendlier town. One where people looked out for one another. Plus, once Greg was in remission, living somewhere with a slower lifestyle would be a good thing. Less stress, more fishing. At least that was how the oncologist put it. It'd be easier for Ruth, too, when it came to caring for her husband. The entire family was willing to relocate since no one was currently married or settled down yet. After all, Durham Security truly was a family-run business.

The timing was perfect. Plus, it gave Greg something else besides his illness to focus on.

"Good, I'm glad to hear it." Cole sat up again and planted his feet on the floor. "Let me know what Asher finds. I'll call tomorrow once I've seen the properties. If there's anything promising, I'll take video."

"Sounds like a plan. Have a good night, Cole."

"You too."

He stood, retrieved his candy bar, and tore open the wrapper.

When Erica's alarm clock went off Tuesday morning, she was tempted to knock it off the side table. Instead, she glared at the red 6:00—the glow making her eyes hurt. She'd had a difficult time going to sleep in the first place because every time she closed her eyes, she either saw the man's face in the SUV or the blood on her son's head.

Once she'd finally drifted off, sleep had been fitful. On top of that, Peter woke up twice thanks to nightmares. Finally, she had him bring in a bunch of blankets and pillows. He crashed on the floor of her room, and they were both able to get a few hours of sleep. Still, she was pretty sure she'd be stumbling through the day.

Erica moved to sit on the edge of the bed, but every muscle in her body screamed in protest. She'd never been in a car accident before and hadn't expected to be this sore. A quick glance over her injured shoulder assured her that it hadn't bled through the bandaging. She'd wait and change it tonight when she would have more time.

She peered down at Peter's sleeping form. Her gaze stalled at the bandage on the side of his head. She'd lost track of how many times she'd said a prayer of thanks that he hadn't been hurt worse.

Last night, she offered to let him stay home another day before returning to school, but he'd insisted he wanted to go, which meant they needed to get a move on.

With a groan, she hauled herself out of bed. Apparently, a car accident had the ability to make her thirty-two years feel more like ninety. "Peter. Hey, honey, it's time to wake up."

Fifteen minutes later, once Erica was dressed and cleaned up and certain that Peter wouldn't go back to sleep, she headed to the dining room to start the coffee and set up the continental breakfast she served during the week.

She soaked in the quiet, punctuated only by the coffee maker and the rustling of plastic as she set out packages of bear claws, cinnamon rolls, Danishes, and apple fritters.

There was a cereal corner, too, with dispensers to make it easier for people to get the right amount. The shredded wheat was less than half full, so she went to the kitchen to retrieve a new box to fill it up with. After that, she put some ice in a small bin and pulled out two different cartons of milk from the fridge. The ice would keep the milk cold for the next hour or so until everyone had eaten breakfast.

Erica had just finished setting everything up when Cole strolled into the room wearing a pair of carpenter-style jeans and a dark green T-shirt with sleeves that hugged his biceps.

He gave her a bright smile, but there was a hint of concern in his eyes. "Good morning. How are you feeling?"

"Like I got into a fight with a tree and lost." When she laughed, a spot in her lower back twinged. "I think I'll be sore for a few days, but it could've been much worse." She looked up when Peter entered the room, a book under one arm.

He got a bowl and filled it with his favorite cereal before sitting at the large wooden table, spoon in one hand and book in the other.

Erica loved that her son chose to carry books with him half the time instead of an electronic device. But it also meant she would have to remind him to eat because there was a high possibility he'd forget once he got lost in the story.

"I take it Peter is going to school today?"

"He's determined. He said his friend, Shawn, would want to see his battle wound." She rolled her eyes.

Cole laughed. "That sounds about right."

Erica thought about driving Peter to school, and her chest tightened. How many times had she made the trip before the incident yesterday? She had no idea, but every single one of them had been uneventful. They'd be fine today. But that didn't mean the nerves weren't there. She would also worry about Peter all day long, wondering if his head was bothering him or if he was feeling more stress than he was letting on. It was silly, but there was no getting around it. The constant worrying was just part of the mom gig.

It was probably better for him to stay busy anyway. If he bummed around the B&B all day, he'd get bored, which would drive her crazy, plus give him more time to think about what happened yesterday.

She wasn't sure how long she'd been staring at her son. When she turned her attention to Cole, she found him still looking at her.

Warmth traveled up her neck and into her cheeks. "Sorry, I guess I'm preoccupied."

"Nothing to apologize for." Cole moved to the food table and chose an apple fritter. "I appreciate the breakfast, by the way. I know everything is pre-packaged during the week, but you obviously go to great lengths to choose quality food. I've been enjoying it."

She didn't get many complaints, but it was the first time someone complimented her on that specifically. Truthfully, she had tried numerous products before choosing what she wanted to serve her guests. "I'm very happy to hear that."

When she'd chosen something herself, and they had both gotten a cup of coffee, she went to sit beside Peter, who barely looked up.

Cole followed and motioned to the chair on her left. "Do you mind if I join you?"

"Not at all." She opened her blueberry Danish. "What time is your appointment with the realtor?"

"At eight-thirty." He pulled his phone out and checked something on the screen then turned it so she could see the list of addresses. "We've got four places to look at, and we're supposed to meet at the first location."

Erica was roughly familiar with three out of four of them. She was about to ask him for some details about his business when the B&B's other guest, Sebastian Rumford, came into the dining room with a newspaper tucked under one arm and a briefcase in the other hand. He tipped an invisible hat to Erica.

"Morning, ma'am."

"Good morning, Mr. Rumford. I hope you had a restful night."

The portly man smiled, his cheeks lifting. "I'm sure glad I decided to stay here instead of the hotel where most of the conference attendees did. I don't like it crowded." He glanced around the small dining room and nodded with satisfaction. "I'll be sorry to leave on Thursday."

That's what Erica liked to hear. Word of mouth was a

powerful advertising tool. "We'll be sorry to see you go, but I'm glad to hear that you've been happy with your stay. Maybe you'll be able to come back for vacation sometime."

"You never know." With that, he grabbed three cinnamon rolls, sat down at the far end of the table, and began to read his newspaper.

It had been three Danishes yesterday morning. Not that she minded. She was pretty sure breakfast was offered at the business conference for attendees. It made her wonder if her continental breakfast was that much better or if he ate just as much at the conference, too.

She put a hand on Peter's shoulder. "When you've finished that, make sure you have your homework in your bag. I've got your lunch in the fridge, so grab that too."

"I will." He scooped the last spoonful of cereal into his mouth and jumped up from his spot, disappearing into the kitchen with his dishes.

Erica shook her head. That boy kept her hopping. She wouldn't have it any other way.

She turned her attention back to Cole, who had finished his breakfast and was pushing his chair away from the table.

He stood and straightened his shirt with a tug. "I'm... uh... sure you've got a full plate today. But if you're free, and it's something you're interested in, I'd appreciate a second set of eyes on these locations."

That was unexpected, and Erica blinked at him for a moment or two. He seemed genuine and maybe a little surprised that he'd asked.

Truthfully, there was very little on her to-do list today. She'd be hanging around the B&B while Bethany took care of everything and counting down the minutes until it was time to pick Peter up from school again.

Going with Cole to check out property sounded much more interesting. "Sure, I could do that."

"That's great." His smile crinkled his dark brown eyes. "Why don't I follow you and Peter to school. That way, you don't have to make the trip back here before we go?"

Just the idea that she wouldn't be driving down the country roads alone was enough to have Erica agree to the suggestion.

Chapter Four

Cole wasn't sure what got into him when he asked Erica if she'd be interested in looking at property with him.

What he did know was that he could truly use a second pair of eyes—someone who knew the area and wasn't trying to make money off a sale.

He also suspected the emotional repercussions from all that happened yesterday were more than she let on.

Chances were, Erica was in the wrong place at the wrong time, and whoever was driving the SUV had a serious case of road rage. But the idea of her driving Peter to school this morning without someone watching her back didn't sit well with him.

So he followed them to Peter's school. Then they'd parked her rental car there and ridden together in his truck. When he offered to drive, she had zero objections.

Now he was behind the wheel with Erica in the passenger seat, and they had over an hour to kill before his appointment. "Can I buy you a coffee to thank you for helping me today?"

Erica chuckled, and the sound made Cole smile.

"After what you did for Peter and me, if anyone should buy someone a coffee, it's me."

"Completely unnecessary. Where do you recommend?"

She gave him directions to a place called Rule the Roast not far from the school. An eagle perched on the edge of a nest was painted on the large front window.

"Clever name." He parked the car. "How's your shoulder?"

Erica shrugged as they walked in. "It'll be fine."

Most of the time, she managed to hide the pain, but Cole had noticed her wince when she got into her car earlier. He wanted to ask if she was staying on top of her painkillers and if she'd need help changing the bandage on her wound, but he didn't feel like it was appropriate.

They ordered their coffee and then found a small table in the corner to drink them.

Erica took a sip and nodded her approval. "What kind of company do you work for? And what kind of places are you guys looking at?"

"I work for a private security company in the San Antonio area. We want to go somewhere a little more remote. Not so busy. Where the local law enforcement might be easier to work with."

Her eyebrows rose in surprise. "So private security as in computer systems? Or protecting people directly?"

"Both. We've had a few customers who wanted us to make sure their business or home was completely impenetrable. But most of the time, our company is hired to protect someone that may be in danger." He took a drink of his coffee. It was good, although he wasn't sure it was all that much better than what Erica was serving at her place.

"And what do you do there? At the company?"

She leaned back in her chair, and Cole could practically see her forming impressions in her mind.

"Personal security. And, apparently, property procurement." He chuckled, hoping to put her at ease.

He wished he knew what she was thinking. Some people felt this line of work was a joke. Others assumed that, if he were hired on as someone's bodyguard, he was all muscle and no brain.

Erica just studied him for several moments. "No wonder you handled things at the accident with such a cool head. How does one get into that particular line of work?"

The only emotion he detected on her face was an honest curiosity.

"It's a family business I was pulled into."

"So not *your* family?" She raised an eyebrow at him.

He chuckled and shook his head. "It's complicated."

She seemed content to wait for him to expand on his explanation.

"Seriously, Erica, you're going to regret asking me."

"I'll take the risk." She lifted her coffee cup to her lips, blue eyes connecting with his over the top of it.

Those eyes. Did she have any idea just how much power they wielded?

"Okay." He cleared his throat. "Long story short, I never knew my father. I don't even know who he is. My mother was... troubled. She couldn't stand doing anything on her own and was always looking for the next man to take care of her." It sounded harsh, but it was true. He'd recognized the reality even as a young boy. "She was into drugs. Alcohol. We moved all the time."

Sadness flitted across Erica's face. She set her cup down. "I'm sorry. You don't have to tell me if you don't want to. I shouldn't have pried."

He gave her a small smile and continued. "I have an older half-brother named Mac who didn't really live with us. My mother and Mac's father weren't together long, and his father insisted on keeping Mac with him. Greg—that's Mac's dad—remarried and went on to have more kids. But when things were bad, my mother would always go to him asking for money."

Cole drained some more of his coffee. "When I was thirteen, she woke me up one night and told me she had to start over. She took me to Mac's house, asked Greg to take me in, and walked away. I never saw her again."

Erica covered her mouth with one hand, tears shining in her eyes. "I can only imagine how hard that was for you."

Even as a teenager, Cole had assumed she'd come back for him. It'd been difficult for him to realize that she'd truly abandoned him. "I knew Mac a little, but not that well. Greg's wife, Ruth, was very upset, as you can imagine. But she was always kind to me. The only familial tie I had was that Mac was my half-brother." He swallowed. Fought to keep his voice even. "Greg and Ruth could have handed me over to the state. Instead, they sought guardianship and brought me into their family. I went from being an only child to having Mac as an older sibling and four younger ones."

"Wow. That was amazing of them."

"It really was." He owed the family everything.

"But you never felt like you fit in." Her words were matter-of-fact.

Cole's eyes widened when she hit the nail on the head. "No. And I realize that's more on me than any of them. But I grew up waiting for my mother to come back and take me away. Or for Greg and his family to change their minds, especially when I wasn't the easiest kid to deal with."

Erica seemed to sense the need to shift their conversation in a different direction. "So how long has the family been in the private security business?"

"Greg built the company with his dad, and the kids each fell into it at different times. Mac knew that's what he wanted to do from the very beginning. For Gavin, it was after he left the military following an injury."

"Impressive. And they sent you here to find a new place to set up shop?" She looked thoughtful as she tapped the lid on her empty cup with the tip of one finger.

"Something like that." He couldn't believe he'd spilled his whole messy history to her in one sitting like that. He almost never talked about it and was already wishing he'd kept his mouth shut. It was about time to head out and meet the realtor. He picked their cups up and took them to the trash. "You ready to go?"

She seemed surprised by the sudden end to the conversation but didn't question it. Instead, she stood with a nod.

Erica got the sense that Cole either didn't usually open up to other people about his childhood, or he regretted that he said anything to her. Either way, their conversation after leaving the coffee shop was centered around meeting the real estate agent, which was fine. She got it. She'd had many instances in the past when she opened up to someone only to regret it later.

Together, they navigated their way to the first property, which was on the other side of town in the business district. A nice car was waiting out front. The moment they pulled up, a woman got out and gave them a wave. She had her hair pulled back and she wore a dark pantsuit with a full smile on her face.

She stuck her hand out toward Cole. "Tanya Lewis. We've spoken on the phone."

"Cole Shepherd. It's nice to meet you." He turned and rested a hand against Erica's back. "This is my friend, Erica Keyes. She's familiar with the area and will be helping me out today."

"Of course. Nice to meet you, too."

Erica shook the realtor's hand, fully aware that Cole's hand hadn't moved an inch. It didn't matter. Not really. But there was something about the gesture that made her feel included. Taken care of.

Which was ridiculous. She intentionally took a subtle step forward as they walked toward the property and put a little space between them.

This particular building ended up being way too industrial. It was huge, with plenty of room to do whatever Cole and his crew might want to do, but it was cold. Empty.

When Cole asked her what she thought, she said as much. To her surprise, he agreed immediately and asked to see the next place.

They removed one option before even seeing it based on Erica's recommendation earlier. The second was way too small. There was a lot of land, but Cole was concerned about the amount of construction that would be needed to even be able to use it.

Which led them to the final property.

"I saved the best for last," Tanya announced as they walked back to their vehicles. "I think it may have everything you're looking for."

Cole held the door open for Erica, then went around and got behind the wheel. "I would have preferred to see it first and save the time," he muttered. But when he looked at Erica, there was an amused smile on her face.

She chuckled. "Where's the fun in that, though? She probably figures, this way, maybe you'll tell a friend or two about the other properties. Two for the price of one." It was a joke, but she probably wasn't too far off.

Instead of starting the truck and immediately following the realtor, Cole watched her for a moment. His face was serious, but there was a warmth in his eyes. "I'm glad I asked you to come with me today."

"I'm glad you did, too." She had to admit she liked the guy. More than she probably should. He was only in town temporarily unless he and the business relocated to Destiny. The thought gave her far more hope than it should have. She hadn't so much as dated since Peter's dad. She didn't have time for that. So why was she entertaining the crazy thought now?

They followed the realtor to the next location. As soon as they pulled into the long driveway, and a huge house came into view, Erica had a good feeling about the place. She glanced at Cole. What was he thinking?

They parked in front of the building and met the realtor at the door. She had a triumphant look on her face. "What do you think?"

"What is this place?"

"It used to be a boys' home. There are ten rooms, six bathrooms, a gym, and an industrial-sized kitchen."

Cole's brows rose. "Let's go inside and take a look."

By the time they finished touring the place, he had decided to take a video to see what the rest of the family wanted to do. The realtor stepped out for a few minutes to give Cole and Erica time to make those recordings and talk.

"This is so perfect, it's almost unreal," he said as he

reviewed some of his video footage. "There's plenty of space for everyone to live here if they wanted to. Guest rooms. I mean, the gym alone would be awesome."

"That's great. It really is an amazing place."

Cole nodded as he looked around them at the room they were standing in. It was one of three common rooms spread throughout the large house. "Some things will need to be updated. The carpet is clearly worn out. I know Ruth will want some changes made to the kitchen. But overall, it looks fabulous."

Once they were back outside, the realtor handed Cole a file with more information, gave them both a card, and said she looked forward to hearing from them soon. She drove away with a wave.

Cole slipped the business card into his wallet and then hefted the stack of papers. "It'll be interesting to see what everyone else says about this place. If it's a no-go, maybe there are a few more properties that I can arrange to see."

"I'm sure there are. But you seem to like it. Surely, that will hold some weight."

"It will. Some." He tilted his head. "I'm trying to decide whether I'm going to stay with Durham Security or not. I can't really be the deciding factor on a location that I may or may not be working at." He laughed with a shake of his head. "I don't know why I keep telling you all this stuff. I'm sorry."

"No apologies needed. Sometimes it helps to talk to someone that you might never see again." Her words sounded casual. Conversational. Inside, though, she was disappointed that he might not be moving to Destiny, which was ludicrous because she barely knew the man.

Cole studied her for several moments until her cell phone began to ring, shattering the silence.

Erica immediately recognized the school's number. "This is Erica."

"Hi, Ms. Keyes. This is Principal Wallace. We had an incident here at the school, and I was wondering if you were free to drop by and discuss it?"

Principal? "Is Peter okay?"

"I assure you everything is fine. But we'd like you to come down if you're able."

Erica stood taller and frowned. "I will definitely be there as soon as I can. Just tell me whether or not my son is hurt."

There was a heartbeat of silence before Principal Wallace responded. "An unknown adult was questioning several of the kids on the playground, including Peter. The man took off before one of our teachers or the resource officer could get there. We're informing each of those children's parents personally and hoping you might recognize the individual from a photograph."

Someone had been bothering her son at his school? An image of the guy in the SUV yesterday flashed through her mind, and she shivered.

Cole gently grasped her elbow and directed her around the truck. "Come on. I'll drive you over there."

Chapter Five

During the entire drive back to the school, Erica fiddled with the trim along the edge of her seat and stared straight ahead. Cole had been able to hear both sides of the conversation, and his impression of her went up another notch when she insisted on knowing the situation surrounding her son.

She seemed a little worried but mostly determined. He wondered if Peter had any idea how blessed he was to have a mom who was ready to take on the world for him.

"It's ridiculous that I had to pull for information about my own son over the phone," she said, her voice tight. "I get maybe they're trying to keep the situation quiet, but not at the expense of informing a parent if something is going on with their kid."

"Agreed." He glanced at Erica's profile before pulling into the school parking lot. "I can wait out here for you, if you'd like. Or I can head on back to the B&B." He didn't know which she preferred, and he didn't want her to feel as though he were trying to push his way into a situation where he didn't belong. He pulled into a parking space next to her car.

Erica released her seatbelt and turned to face him. "On the off chance this is connected to yesterday, would you mind coming in with me? If they have a photo or video, and a vehicle is included, you might recognize it." Even as she said the words, it was clear she was second-guessing herself. "Never mind. I'm sure you have all kinds of information to go through before you talk to the family. You should head back. Hopefully this won't take long."

"Erica." He waited for her to stop talking and look at him again. "I'm happy to go in with you."

She didn't smile, but she did nod, and her shoulders relaxed a little.

When they entered the school, Erica checked in at the main office. They didn't have time to sit before someone escorted them down several halls to an office with Principal Simon Wallace written on the door.

A tall, thin man in his fifties greeted them and motioned for them to sit down. "Thank you for coming on such short notice." He extended a hand toward Cole and introduced himself.

"Cole Shepherd. Nice to meet you."

"Cole is a friend who's in town for a few days," Erica explained.

"Well, as you know, we have many precautions in place to assure the safety of our students, and that includes on the playground." The principal looked at Cole. "The play-ground itself is fenced. There are never fewer than four adults out there with the kids."

"So what exactly happened?" Erica folded her hands and rested them on her lap. She looked relaxed, but Cole noted that her knuckles were white.

He nearly reached over to cover her hands with his but stopped himself.

"Peter was on the playground playing with a couple of friends. They were kicking the ball back and forth. From what I understand, the ball was kicked away from the group toward the fence. When the boys ran over to retrieve it, a man stepped up to the fence and started talking to them." He pulled up something on his laptop and turned it around, revealing a very grainy picture of a man who was wearing a hoodie. "Apparently, he asked the boys multiple questions about their favorite foods, toys, and video games."

Erica leaned forward and studied the photo. "It's hard to see, but there's nothing about him that's familiar."

Between the grainy image and the hoodie, it was impossible to really make out a face. Cole agreed. He didn't recognize the individual.

The principal gave a satisfied nod. "Apparently, Peter informed the man that they weren't allowed to talk to strangers, and they had started to leave the fence line when one of the teachers noticed the exchange. The man ran off before the teacher was able to speak with him." He turned the laptop around again and pulled up a video.

The quality of the video wasn't any better than the image, but the man could be seen jogging off screen.

"Is there any footage of the vehicle he got into?" Cole asked.

"Unfortunately, there isn't. It was parked far enough away that the teachers on the playground couldn't see it." The principal closed the laptop. "We did commend the boys—and Peter in particular—for not answering the stranger's questions. I will be instructing all classes to go over basic safety rules and guidelines with their students this week. You can never be too careful."

"I'm glad to hear that." Erica seemed pleased with the principal's praise. "I'll speak with Peter about it when he's home from school too. Can I ask which boys were with him?"

"Shawn and Axel. I'm going to be speaking with their parents as well. If an identification is made, I'll be sure to let you know."

"Thank you so much."

Principal Wallace stood, and Cole and Erica followed suit. "Thank you again for coming in." He shook their hands and led them back to the front office.

As they left the school, Cole took in the parking lot with new eyes. It had an open layout with several entrances. It would be impossible for the school to completely close it off or monitor everyone who came in and left.

"You should be proud of Peter. It sounds like he handled himself well."

The corners of Erica's lips lifted. "I am. It's nice to know all those conversations we've had stuck." The smile didn't last long. "Sounds like it was random. Like it just happened to be Peter and his friends who ran to the fence, and it could've been any of the kids."

"Yeah, it does." There was no reason in the world to connect yesterday's events with the creep at the playground today. He could certainly understand why she might be unnerved, though, and he didn't blame her one bit. "I guess it's time to head back to the B&B. Thanks for going with me to see the properties."

"Thank *you* for going with me to see the principal." Erica raised a brow. "Bet you didn't see getting called in to the principal's office coming when you chose to stay at my B&B." A soft chuckle softened the worry on her face.

Cole was quickly becoming fond of the sound of her

laughter. "I have to admit, it's been a much more adventurous trip than I expected." And it was probably good that he was going to be leaving again. It would be way too easy to get attached to both Erica and her son. The sooner he got back to normal, the better.

Sometime later, once he'd eaten dinner with Erica, Peter, and the other guest, he settled in his room and called Mac. His success must have shown on his face because Mac grinned.

"I take it you found something?"

"It's almost perfect. Like, there must be a catch perfect. Hold on, let me send you the videos and photos."

By the time Mac had received them, Greg and Ruth had joined him along with Asher. Cole didn't know where the rest of the Durham clan was, but if the others agreed the property was a good choice, the footage would be shown to everyone else.

Mac let out a low whistle. "You're not kidding. How long has the place been sitting there empty?"

Cole went through everything with them. Inspections would need to be done, and Greg had a few questions for the realtor. But the property had a lot of potential. Enough that the family agreed he should meet with the realtor with a few more questions, and they would go from there.

In other words, he'd be free to head home in the next day or two.

Cole pictured his apartment. It was in a building with neighbors he didn't know. It was such a small thing, eating meals with everyone here at the B&B, but it made him realize how much he missed that.

"Hey, Asher. Did you get a chance to check into Erica Keyes?"

The youngest Durham—well, tied for youngest with his

twin sister Olivia—moved onto the screen. "Hey. Yeah, nothing unusual there. She's thirty-two, has a son, owns the Tranquil Bed and Breakfast, although the bank still holds the lien, and her record is squeaky clean. I'm talking nothing but a lone parking ticket." He ran his fingers through his short hair that ended in curls.

"You didn't see anything that would explain why she might be targeted?"

"Not a thing."

Mac came back onto the screen, squeezing in beside Asher. "Did something else happen?"

"Some guy was asking her son and his friends some creepy leading questions at school before he was run off. No ID. Probably a coincidence."

"But your Spidey senses are tingling." It was a joke, but Asher said it with a serious face because Cole's intuition was something they'd learned to pay attention to long ago.

Not that he was always right, but his instincts were spot on more often than not.

Cole shrugged in a way that he hoped looked casual. "I just wanted to cover the bases before I leave Destiny. It's one thing if she's had a run of bad luck. It's another to walk away if she and her son are in trouble."

In an instant, Erica Keyes went from being sound asleep to completely awake early Wednesday morning. The moment her son's face came into focus, she startled and pressed a hand to her chest. "Peter! You scared me." She pushed herself into a sitting position in her bed. "What's the matter, honey?"

"There was a weird noise outside my window." Even

though the only light in her room came from the streetlight filtering through the curtains and the red glow from the alarm clock on her nightstand, it was easy to see Peter was frightened.

Erica glanced at the clock. Nearly four in the morning.

A scratching noise pulled her attention to the window in her bedroom. Peter jumped over Erica and onto the bed beside her. "A noise like that."

"Okay." She reached over and gave his hand a squeeze. He was right, though. The sound was an odd one. There weren't any tree branches or bushes close enough to either of their windows for them to brush against the panes. "You stay right here. I'm going to see what's going on."

Peter climbed under the covers and gave a quick nod.

Erica was used to being a single mom, and she took care of nearly everything that her son or her business needed. What she couldn't handle, her dad or Bryce would step in and assist with. She was blessed to have them in her life.

Most of the time, she felt confident in being single. And then there were moments like these when she desperately wished for a husband.

Ignoring the aches and pains in her body, she snatched her socks off the floor and slid them onto her feet. The cool air cut right through her cotton pajama pants and T-shirt, so she got her sweatshirt from the top of her dresser and pulled that on. "Remember, stay here."

Another moment of listening in the silence revealed no more odd noises. She contemplated sneaking to the window and looking out, and then she imagined a creepy creature or person lurking on the other side. She opted to scare whatever it was away first.

Erica got a flashlight out of the nightstand drawer and walked over to the window.

Cautiously, she pulled the curtain away from one side, peered out, and turned the flashlight on. Nothing but the dark side yard. No red eyes staring at her or rabid animals. A quick check reassured her that the window was still locked.

She released a lungful of air that she didn't realize she'd been holding and walked over to the light switch. "Watch your eyes." She flicked the light on and flinched momentarily against the brightness.

"I'm going to go check the other rooms. I'll be right back."

"Maybe we should call Uncle Bryce."

It was tempting. He was on duty tonight, too. But she wasn't about to call him because of an odd noise, even if she knew he would be there in moments. "We're okay, honey. It was probably a squirrel or raccoon or something."

Peter nodded but didn't look convinced.

Erica exited her bedroom and entered the hallway of their little apartment area. When she'd first bought it after Peter had turned four, she'd had some construction done so they could have their own living area with a bathroom and two bedrooms.

With the flashlight still in one hand, she turned the lights on in the living area before checking the bathroom and finally Peter's room. Just like before, she cautiously looked out his bedroom window and shined a flashlight.

Part of her was relieved that there was nothing unusual to see. The other part would always wonder what made the sound.

Back in her bedroom, she joined Peter on the bed and reached for her phone. They had a security camera aimed at the front door outside, another at the back door, and then one in the main entrance to the B&B. Thanks to an app on her phone, Erica could check the footage from her room.

Or she should have been able to.

According to her phone, the Wi-Fi was out, which meant the cameras were currently offline.

A shiver slid down her spine. She really wanted to say everything was fine and tell Peter he could go back to sleep, but now she was concerned about making sure the main doors were locked.

She swallowed a sigh. "I'm going to go check the rest of the house. I want you to stay right here. You can lock my bedroom door behind me if you want to. I'll come right back."

Peter looked like he wanted to argue with her. Instead, he got out of bed. "Be careful, Mom."

"I will." She smiled and pressed a kiss to his forehead where the bandage remained. "I'm sure it was just the wind. I have my phone, my flashlight, my keys, and you know what Uncle Bryce says, right?"

Peter grinned. "That he pities anyone crazy enough to mess with you."

"That's right. Don't open the door until you hear me talking to you on the other side."

She waited to hear the click of the lock and then exited their apartment area before locking that door as well. All the other bedrooms in the B&B were upstairs.

Further down the hall, she turned the corner and was about to flip the light on for the main room when her focus was drawn to the large double window that was illuminated by the streetlight outside. A shadow passed in front of it.

Erica froze.

Feeling vulnerable, she considered backing out of the

room and leaving. But then she thought about Peter and her other guests. She withdrew her phone, ready to dial for help.

Chapter Six

The shadow Erica thought she saw morphed into a man standing in the room near the door. She yelped and flipped on the living room lights. The man spun around.

"Cole?" The relief that flooded Erica when she recognized him was immediately followed by suspicion. "Why are you wandering around in the dark?"

His eyes widened. "I didn't mean to startle you. I had trouble sleeping and thought I'd see if there was any coffee left from yesterday. I had just come downstairs when I heard a noise at the front door." He cast a look in that direction. "I hope I didn't wake you."

"No." She hesitated. "I was coming to make sure the doors were locked because there was a noise outside our windows and the Wi-Fi is down, so I can't check the security cameras outside."

His eyebrows rose. "Maybe I should go check the perimeter. Make sure no one is lurking around outside."

There was something comforting about the thought that he was willing to do that. She considered taking him up on it, but it was dark outside, and he wouldn't be able to see much anyway. They might as well wait for daylight.

"If there was anyone out there, I'm sure my turning on all the lights would have deterred them. Besides, this is Texas. It was probably the wind."

Cole chuckled. "Probably so." He didn't look completely convinced but seemed willing to let it go. "Why don't I go double-check the back door? It's through the utility room if I remember correctly."

"Yes. Thank you."

While he did that, she turned the lights on in the kitchen and dining room. Everything seemed to be in its place. Cole returned a minute later to say the same was true for the back door.

Erica turned the flashlight off and slipped her phone back into her pocket. "Peter is awake and worried. Let me go tell him everything is okay. Then I'll come back and start some coffee."

He checked his watch. "It's still early. You might have time to get a little more rest."

"Not going to happen." There was no way she could relax enough to fall back to sleep. She studied the handsome man standing in front of her. "You're welcome to get some more sleep, though. Otherwise, there'll be a cup of coffee with your name on it shortly."

A slightly crooked smile brightened his face and caused a shallow dimple to appear on each cheek. "I appreciate that. If you'll show me where the coffee is, I can get that started while you check on Peter."

She led the way to the dining area and showed him where the canister of coffee was in the cabinet below the coffee maker. "I'll be back in a few minutes."

He gave her a slight nod and turned his attention to the appliance.

Erica headed back to their apartment. Only as she was unlocking the door did she realize she'd been talking to Cole in her pajama pants and sweatshirt. Heat flooded her cheeks.

"As if it really matters," she chided herself in a whisper.

Back at her bedroom door, she knocked softly. "Peter. It's me, I'm coming in."

She opened the door and found her son right where she left him. "Everything is fine. I think it was just the wind."

He nodded drowsily, his face relaxing with relief.

"Do you think you can go back to sleep?" Erica sat on the edge of her bed and ran a hand over her son's head.

"Yeah." He yawned.

"Okay. Why don't you stay here, and I'll come wake you up when it's time to get up and get ready for school."

Peter nodded again and shifted until his head was resting on the pillow. His lashes fluttered and fell against his cheeks. "Will you leave the light on?"

"Of course." Erica's heart swelled. Being a single parent was far from easy, but Peter was worth it. Worth everything.

She thought about the scare earlier and shivered. There was one thing she had no doubt about: She would do anything to protect her son.

◎

Cole watched Erica leave the kitchen before he tackled the coffee maker. He couldn't help but notice her pajama pants with dogs and hearts printed all over them. Between those and the sweatshirt, she'd looked entirely too adorable.

After everything she'd been through this week, when

she heard a noise, she'd been willing to come down and check the doors by herself. Seriously, the woman was a force to be reckoned with. Add to that the fact that she was kind, attentive to her guests, and a caring mom to Peter, and it seemed like she was the perfect combination.

A dangerous combination.

He'd never imagined himself to be a family man. He still didn't. But there was something about Erica that made him wish he could be.

The coffee maker came to life, and Cole breathed in the aroma. He looked forward to a cup of coffee, although the adrenaline from earlier still hadn't faded completely.

All of that was on top of not resting well. No matter what he did, he couldn't get his mind quiet enough to fall asleep for long. If everything worked out, and the Durhams purchased the property he found, then he had a decision to make. Was he moving to Destiny with everyone else? Staying in the San Antonio area? Or going somewhere else entirely?

The possibilities, in combination with the day he spent with Erica, made it impossible to sleep.

After dozing off and on for a while, he'd decided to come downstairs and walk around. He'd been hoping a change of scenery would be enough to help him go to sleep once he'd gone back upstairs.

And then he'd heard a sound at the front door.

At first, it was a scratching noise. He'd wondered if a dog was on the other side hoping someone would open the door and give it some food. Until the doorknob rattled as though someone was testing to see if it was locked.

He was just about to see if someone was lurking on the porch when the lights came on. He hadn't expected to find

Erica standing there—and in those adorable pajamas, no less —when he turned around.

He had a feeling she would've gone toe-to-toe with him if he had been an intruder.

According to her, she'd heard noises outside her window. Combine that with the front door and the fact that the Wi-Fi had gone out at the same time, and it made Cole more than a little suspicious. As soon as it was light enough, he had every intention of going outside and looking around the perimeter of the B&B.

A handful of minutes later, Erica re-entered the dining area. Apparently, she lived on coffee like he did. He imagined her as a cartoon character floating through the air as she followed the scent. He covered his smile with one hand.

Erica poured coffee into a cup and handed it to Cole before getting another for herself.

"Is Peter okay?"

She added sugar and a flavored creamer to her coffee before stirring it. "He seems to be. He's going back to sleep for a while." She took a sip and hummed her satisfaction.

Cole typically drank his coffee black, and a sip of his own brew had him agreeing with her assessment. It was a particularly good batch. "I didn't notice what kind of coffee this was. It's really good."

Erica got the canister back out and handed it to him. "I was first introduced to it by Tia at the police department. For a long time, she refused to reveal her source. But I guess she finally decided it was only fair to share the secret. They really should give her a commission on all the sales her endorsements have led to."

He took note of the brand. "Sounds like they should." He took another sip and set it down at the table before claiming a chair. "What inspired you to take on a bed and breakfast?"

She looked thoughtful, as though she were trying to decide how much she wanted to share with him.

"It was mostly a means to an end." She paused. "My husband and I divorced before Peter was born. I lived with my parents for the first couple of years, worked full time, and saved everything I could." She sat down across from him and cupped her coffee mug with both hands. "I wanted to eventually work somewhere to support my son and be more independent. When the original owner of this place put it up for sale, it seemed like the perfect opportunity." She shrugged as if it were no big deal.

Except it was. Cole knew first-hand what it was like to have parents who didn't think their family was worth putting in the effort for. Erica never gave up on her son. "Good for you. You have a lot to be proud of. I'm sorry to hear about the divorce, though. Does Peter's father spend much time with him?"

Erica took another swallow of her coffee. "He's never met Peter. He wasn't interested."

Cole's jaw tightened. He had no idea what led to the divorce, so it was difficult to judge. Although from what he knew of Erica already, anyone who walked away from her was a fool. But to not be interested in his own son? "I realize I've only known you for a few days, but I can say with certainty that it's your ex's loss."

With a slight dip of her chin, Erica said, "Yes, it is. Thank you." She gave a little shrug. "Sometimes life doesn't turn out the way we thought it would. But there are always highlights when we look for them. Things that remind us that there's more good than bad, you know?"

Cole let her words settle over him. She was right, of

course. She made it sound so simple, while he found that he tended to focus on the negative side of things. Her positivity made him want to do better.

His mug had a map of Texas printed on it with Destiny highlighted. He ran his thumb over the slightly raised star.

Erica cleared her throat. "There are a lot of different directions you could have taken after all that happened with your parents. But you chose to work in a field where you help others. That's admirable, Cole."

That was about the last thing he expected her to say. "I appreciate that."

Working for Durham Security had simply happened. There'd been no selfless inclination there. He'd needed a job, and he knew what he was getting into with the Durham family. But helping people? He'd found it fit his personality. His need to find order in a situation where there was none.

Their conversation lulled for several moments. Cole used a thumbnail to lightly flick at a spot on the mug where the Texas outline was coming away from the ceramic. When he looked up again, he found Erica watching him. Curiosity and something else flashed in her eyes before she stood.

"I'd better go get a few things done before I wake up Peter." She topped her coffee cup off.

"Thanks again for the coffee." He stood as well. "As soon as it's light enough, I'll go outside and look around. Make sure someone didn't mess with the place."

"Not necessary, but I appreciate it." With a smile and a nod, she left the kitchen.

Cole sat down again to finish his coffee.

Once the sun had risen enough, the first thing he did was inspect the front door. There was nothing to see, though. No sign that someone had tried to force their way in.

He walked around the building to the side where the windows were for Erica's apartment area. The trees needed a trim as they were getting close to the house, but none of the branches touched the building.

Then something caught his eye. He got closer and looked at the ground. The grass had been trampled, and there were shoeprints in the mud. He wasn't sure which room this was.

Cole got his phone out and took several photos before getting closer and rising to his toes to get a better look at the window. The screen in one corner had been lifted slightly away from the frame. It could be an old screen. Or the damage might be new.

Based on the small, colorful robot sticker on the bottom right of the windowpane, he assumed this must be Peter's room.

The idea that anyone might be trying to look in on the boy, much less break into the room, had Cole clenching his fist. He was thankful for the weight of the .45 nestled against his back. He'd like to run into the creeper right now.

Cole moved to the next window. He had to assume it was Erica's room, although the blue curtains on the other side of the blinds made it impossible to know for sure. Just like with Peter's window, the ground had been stomped and grass flattened just below. The screen looked untouched, though.

A tour around the rest of the exterior revealed nothing else noteworthy.

Which meant one of two things—either it was a coincidence that the two windows happened to be Erica and

Peter's rooms, or the creeper knew exactly which rooms they stayed in.

Chapter Seven

Erica hadn't actually expected Cole to find anything when he checked the perimeter. The idea that someone was trying to look inside Peter's window... Goosebumps peppered her arms, and she rubbed at them through the sleeves of her shirt. "It doesn't mean that they were trying to look at us. Maybe they were just the first two windows they tried, and when we turned the lights on, it was enough of a deterrence."

"That's a definite possibility," Cole leaned against the edge of the counter in the kitchen.

As soon as she had returned with Peter in tow, he'd asked to speak to her privately. Erica made sure Peter was set with breakfast and then agreed.

"But you're not convinced."

Cole pushed away from the counter. "It's not that. What you said might very well be true. But I do find it suspicious that the Wi-Fi went out at the same time." He cleared his throat. "Do you mind if I take a look at the footage and see how long it was out?"

Erica hesitated, then decided there wasn't any harm.

She withdrew her phone, pulled up the app, and handed it to him. "It only records when there's movement. There may not be a way to tell."

With the skills of someone who worked in the security field, he opened some settings in the app, scrolled down, and turned the phone around to show her. "It was out for less than fifteen minutes."

She took the phone back and scanned the logs. He was right. It was timed perfectly so that the cameras wouldn't capture anyone who might have been messing with the windows or the front door. "Someone used a signal jammer."

Cole's eyes widened. He seemed surprised she even knew what one was. "That's my guess as well."

"Is there any way to verify that?"

"Not easily, no."

"Then it could technically be a coincidence." Although Erica doubted it. "Maybe someone was casing the area. Looking for homes and businesses to break into in the future. Hopefully the fact that you and I both responded will get the B&B crossed off the list of potential targets."

Cole offered her a reassuring smile. "Hopefully so. Still, it might not be a bad idea to mention it to the police. Just in case someone else in the neighborhood had similar problems. I took photos of the two locations. Would you like me to send them to you? I should still have your number from calling your phone after your accident."

"That would be great, thank you."

Moments later, her own phone pinged as the pictures came through.

She glanced at the photos and then added his phone number to her contacts. "These are great. I'll send them to

Jenny. Let her know what happened after I get Peter to school."

"I can follow you guys into town if you'd like."

As tempting as it was to take him up on the offer, she couldn't have someone escort her to town every day for the foreseeable future. Even if the idea of driving that stretch of road on her own made her nervous. "I appreciate it. But I'm sure you've got all kinds of things you need to get done without having to babysit Peter and me."

One of his eyebrows rose. "First, it's far from babysitting. Secondly, I'm planning to stop by the realtor's office first thing this morning. So I'm heading that way anyway. Besides, I work in private security, remember? You'd be doing me a favor by making sure my skills don't get rusty while I'm staying in Destiny."

He smiled then, his dimples flashing into view.

Erica gave him a look to show him that she knew exactly what he was doing. "Well, in that case, I'll be happy to share the road with you." Did that sound too much like flirting? She cleared her throat. "I'd better make sure Peter's got everything he needs for school today. After not sleeping well the last two nights, he's dragging."

"How about you? How are you doing with everything?" His gaze went to her injured shoulder. "This can't be easy for you either."

"It hasn't been. But we'll get through it. We always do." She rubbed the sore spot on her shoulder. With everything else going on, there hadn't been a lot of time to worry about it.

"Well, let me know when you're ready to head out."

Erica got the impression he wanted to say more than that and wondered what it was that he was holding back.

She got Peter's lunch ready, helped him double-check

that he had his homework, and then glanced at her watch. Normally, Bethany would have been here by now. Thankfully, Mr. Rumford had already left for his conference, which meant it shouldn't be a big deal if Erica had to close and lock the B&B while she took Peter to school.

"I'm ready, Mom." Peter adjusted his backpack and shifted from one foot to the other. "Where's Bethany?"

"I don't know, honey. Let me give her a call quick." Cole joined them as she dialed Bethany's number. It rang once and then went straight to voicemail. Erica frowned and left a voice message before hanging up. "All right, we need to get going. I'll go ahead and lock the B&B. Chances are, she'll get here just as we're leaving." Bethany had her own set of keys anyway.

Hopefully she was feeling okay. Erica knew several people who had come down with colds or the flu in the last week. It was way too early in the fall for all the illnesses to hit.

Cole followed Erica in his truck all the way to the school. From that point, he gave them a wave and drove off.

After dropping Peter off, Erica tried Bethany's number again but got her voicemail like before. If she wasn't at the B&B, Erica had better get back.

She dialed Bryce's number once she'd left the school zone.

"Hey, Erica. How's it going?"

"I wasn't sure if you'd still be sleeping or not."

Bryce was off today, but sometimes, if Megan had an early shift at the hospital, he slept in for a while to get caught up. With weird schedules like they had, the two of them did everything they could to spend quality time together when they weren't working.

"A smoke alarm started going off at six this morning. Ironic, right?"

Erica pictured her brother using the large ladder on a firetruck at the station to reach the smoke alarm in his own house and chuckled. "Sorry. That stinks. They always pick the worst time to need a new battery."

"That they do. So, what's up?"

"It looks like we had someone prowling around the B&B last night. We got some photos, and I'm going to send them to Jenny when I get back. I thought I might send them to you, too, to see what you think."

"How about I head over there, and you can show me in person?" There were shuffling noises in the background.

There was no sense in arguing with him. Besides, he was probably already in his car and backing out of the driveway. "Thanks, Bryce. We'll probably get there at about the same time. See you in a few."

Twenty minutes later, Erica took the opportunity to join Bryce and check out the evidence herself. The trampled grass was even more obvious in person. She looked from the spot on the ground to her son's window.

"I made sure the windows were locked. I'm seriously considering running down to buy those alarms that go off when the window is opened. Am I overreacting?"

"Nope." Bryce pivoted and led the way to the front of the B&B. "I was just thinking the same thing. This place is big enough, you can't possibly keep an eye on everything. Especially at night." He frowned. "I know you can't, but I wish you and Peter would go to Dad and Mom's place for a few days. Since they're still on vacation, you'd have the place to yourself."

"I'm not going to lie. It's tempting. But I refuse to throw Cole and Mr. Rumford out like that." Guests this time of the year were not nearly as frequent as she would like them to be. She couldn't afford to lose the business by asking them to leave early.

It was clear Bryce wasn't surprised by her answer. "Why don't you give Jenny a call? I'll go through and see how many window alarms you need, and I'll run down and grab those. I have plenty of time this morning to help you get them installed."

Erica gave him a relieved smile. "You're my favorite brother. I hope you know that."

"And don't you forget it."

When Cole got back to the B&B to find a police car parked in the circular driveway, he was immediately concerned. He'd only been at the realtor's office for an hour and a half. He jumped out of his truck and jogged to the front door.

Inside, he spotted Erica's brother on a stepladder by the large windows up front and headed that direction. Once he got close, he recognized the window alarms and nodded his approval. "That's a great idea. You need any help?"

"This is the last one." Bryce activated it and got down. "Thanks, though. We put them on all the downstairs windows. This weekend, once you and the other guest have checked out, we'll probably put them on the second-floor windows as well."

"It certainly doesn't hurt." He jabbed a thumb at the police car they could see through the window. "Is everything okay?"

"Erica called Jenny at the police station about the footprints. She wanted to see everything firsthand and file an official report. They're talking in the kitchen." Bryce studied Cole for several moments before speaking again. "I appreciate you looking out for Erica. I wish I could convince her to take Peter and go somewhere more secure for a few days. But she's stubborn."

Cole fought to keep his smile contained. "You won't hear me argue that point. But it's not necessarily a bad thing."

"When we were kids, it was brutal. But I would agree with you. It's a trait that's helped her through a lot." Bryce took a seat on the top rung of the stepladder. "I hear you work private security and that your company is looking to relocate to Destiny."

"Did Erica tell you that?" He wouldn't be surprised. The siblings seemed close.

"She did. And a thorough background check confirmed it."

Cole gave him a nod of respect. He would have run a background check on himself, too, if he were Bryce. "We think Destiny may be the perfect place for Durham Security. It's important to have a good working relationship with local law enforcement."

"It certainly helps. How long are you planning on staying in town this trip?"

"I originally intended to head back on Friday, but I may delay my return for another day or two." Cole had a feeling he'd need to speak to the realtor at least one more time. More than anything, though, he didn't like the idea of leaving Erica and Peter quite yet.

Bryce straightened again. "I do feel better knowing that she won't be here alone once the other guest checks out on Thursday." He reached into his wallet and pulled out a card. "I'd appreciate it if you kept in touch. You know, if anything like what happened this morning happens again."

"Will do." Cole took one of his own cards out of his wallet and handed it over.

They shook hands, and Bryce led the way to the kitchen where they heard the women still talking in low voices. They both looked up.

"All of the security alarms are on the windows," Bryce announced. "Make sure to tell Peter not to open any of them, or it'll give him the fright of his life. They are loud."

"Good. If anyone messes with a window, I want it to scare them away." Erica stood and gave her brother a hug. "You're the best. Thank you."

Cole turned his attention to Officer Durant. "Did you guys ever find the SUV that ran Erica off the road?"

"Unfortunately, we didn't. Chances are, they left the area immediately after the incident." The officer pushed her chair away from the small table in the corner of the kitchen. "We'll have patrols go by regularly every night for the next week or two. Give us a call if any of you see or hear anything."

Cole's phone rang then, and he excused himself and took it upstairs. Over the next few hours, he went back and forth between the realtor and Greg, getting all the information needed to make a decision. In the end, Greg made an offer on the old boys' ranch. Now they would wait to see whether the owners accepted the lower offer.

Cole suspected Greg intended to counter if they didn't. But since the property had been on the market for over a year, the realtor thought there was a good chance that the offer would go through.

Too bad Cole wasn't as certain about his own future.

Unwilling to explore that any further at the moment, he turned his thoughts to Erica. On the surface, being run off the side of the road, the man talking to Peter at school, and then the prowler outside didn't seem to be connected. But it made no sense for all of it to be happening at the same time.

Except what if it wasn't all about Erica? She wasn't the only one staying at the B&B. He picked up his phone and dialed Asher's number.

"Hey. What's up, Cole?"

"Can you run a background check on someone else for me?" Cole gave him Rumford's information. "He's in town for some business conference and staying at the B&B. See what kind of business he's into and if there's anything shady that we should be worried about." It annoyed him that he hadn't thought to check into the guy in the first place.

Chapter Eight

Bethany didn't show up to work in the afternoon either. Erica had tried not to worry too much that morning. After all, Bethany had her hands full with work and college classes, even if the no-show was unusual.

Now, Erica wished she'd listened to her gut before. She tried to call Bethany again, only to be sent straight to voicemail. What if something was wrong? What if Bethany was sick, or she had fallen and hurt herself? Erica knew very little about the younger woman's family. Did she have anyone local that Erica could call to check on her?

When Erica originally hired her, there were forms to fill out and information to gather. She went to the locked file cabinet in her bedroom and pulled out Bethany's personal details. There were no emergency numbers included—and Erica made a mental note to ask for that from employees in the future—but at least now she had an address.

She dialed Bryce's number. "Hey, little brother. I have a huge favor to ask of you."

Cole came downstairs then. He went to retrieve a bottle of water from a basket in the dining area and left a dollar bill in the coffee can beside it. Then he sat down and started to look through a newspaper.

"Another one? I'm going to have to start keeping track." There was humor in Bryce's words.

"I can't say I'd blame you. I'm pretty sure I owe you a lot over the years. Would you be able to swing by and pick up Peter from school and bring him here? Bethany didn't come in for work this afternoon either."

"Of course. It's not a problem at all. That's unusual for Bethany. Have you tried calling her?"

"Yes, but it just goes straight to voicemail. I thought about going by her place, but I didn't want to overstep. I'm a little worried about her. I'm really hoping she'll reach out this evening or tomorrow morning."

"I hope so, too. I'm sorry that means you don't have any help this afternoon."

Erica glanced at Cole. "It's okay. It's not like the place is hopping right now, anyway. Thanks again, Bryce. I appreciate you. I'll see you guys in a bit."

Erica's parents, Bryce, and Megan were all authorized to pick up Peter. She was glad their parents were enjoying their trip, but their absence now made her realize just how much they did help with everything.

She glanced at her phone, as though there would suddenly be a call or text from Bethany, and then slid it into her pocket with a sigh.

Cole folded the newspaper, placed it on the coffee table. and stood. "If you'll give me Bethany's address, I can swing by her place. See if her car is out front or if anyone is home."

The offer was unexpected. Erica's first reaction was to

thank him and say no. But she hadn't been able to get Bethany out of her mind all day.

"Are you sure it won't be taking you away from something else you need to do?"

"Not at all. I've been on the phone or the computer all afternoon. I could use a change of scenery anyway."

Erica wrote down the address, Bethany's full name, and a description of the younger woman's car, then handed over the paper. "I appreciate it, Cole. Thank you so much."

"You're welcome. Hopefully she's at home with a cold or something and just didn't realize she was sleeping the day away." He gave her an encouraging smile.

"I really hope you're right."

Cole plugged Bethany's address into his phone and followed the directions until he pulled up in front of a townhouse. Bethany's car was not in the driveaway, but another car was.

He got out and walked up the pathway to the door and rang the doorbell.

A minute later, another young woman opened the door and gave him a cautious once-over. "Can I help you?"

"Hi, my name is Cole Shepherd." He held out a hand.

"Lynn." She grasped his hand and gave it a firm shake.

"Is this where Bethany Massy lives?"

"She does. We're roommates."

"I'm helping Erica Keyes out this afternoon. She's the owner of the Tranquil Bed & Breakfast where Bethany works. Bethany never showed up for work today, and she hasn't answered her phone. Erica was worried that Bethany might be sick since this is very unusual for her. Is she here, by chance?"

Cole looked beyond the woman at the door, but it was difficult to see anything past her.

"No, she's not. She left first thing this morning. I haven't seen her since. It's not unusual, though. Sometimes she goes to work, heads over to the community college and stays there until she goes back to work again." Concern flashed in Lynn's eyes. "For Bethany to miss work... it's very unusual.

"What do you mean?"

"Bethany has one of the best work ethics I've ever seen. Almost to a fault, sometimes. Like, even if she's sick, she makes sure she gets all her homework done. She can be up all night studying, but she'll still get to work on time because it's what she committed to do."

"Did she seem concerned this morning? Or act any differently than normal?"

Lynn thought for a moment. "She really didn't. Like I said, there are days I don't see her back here until seven-thirty or eight at night. You might check the community college and see if she's there."

"Do you happen to know which classes she's signed up for?"

"Statistics and chemistry. I couldn't tell you when they were, though. I know, bad roommate." She frowned. "I really hope she's okay. If you see her, will you please tell her to give me a call?"

"I will. And if she comes home, will you let me know or have her call Erica?" He handed her one of his cards. "Thank you so much for your help."

With a nod of his head, Cole turned and walked back to his truck. Once inside, he dialed Erica's phone number. She picked up after the first ring.

"Bethany hasn't been back to the house, but she did leave first thing this morning like she normally does. I'm going to swing by the community college. Check with a professor or two. Then I'll head back to the B&B."

"I appreciate it, Cole. Thank you."

"Not a problem."

Once on campus, he was not surprised to find that the lady at the registrar's office was reluctant to give him Bethany's class schedule, which he could respect. So instead of trying to get any more information that way, he found the building where many of the teacher's offices were and located the math department. There, he inquired about Bethany's statistics class.

"I'm sorry, we aren't able to give out any personal information like that."

"I understand. I know that Bethany had a statistics class today. All I want to do is talk to her teacher and get confirmation that she did attend the class. Do you know if that instructor is still on campus?"

The woman at the main office desk looked hesitant, but she looked some information up before nodding slowly. "Yes, Professor Davis is still here. You can find his office just down the hall. Room 115."

"Thank you." He walked down the hall and was relieved to find Professor Davis sitting at his desk in his office. Cole knocked on the open doorframe.

Davis looked up. "Can I help you?"

"Yes, I was wondering if you could tell me whether one of your students was in class today. A Bethany Massy?"

"She is one of my students, but I did not see her in class today. I think it may be the first time all semester." Davis gave him a curious look. "Why do you ask?"

"I'm sure it's nothing. But she didn't show up for either

of her work shifts, and when she couldn't reach her on the phone, her boss became concerned. We were hoping she got caught up here on campus." Cole was already happy with how much Davis had helped, so he was surprised when the professor offered to reach out to Bethany's other professors and see if she was missing from their classes today as well.

Twenty minutes later, Cole left campus convinced that Bethany had never made it there this morning.

When he got back to the B&B, Bryce and Peter were just arriving.

The boy had jumped out of his uncle's truck with the energy that only young boys can possess. "Hi, Mr. Shepherd!"

"Hey, Peter. Did you have a good day at school?"

"Sure did. Look what my teacher gave me for getting an A in spelling last week!" He held out a patch in the shape of a colorful book. I can't wait to add it to my backpack. I'm starving!" With that, he disappeared into the B&B at a run.

Bryce shook his head. "I can hardly keep up with him. I'm wondering if my son is going to have that much energy when he's that age." There was no missing the look of excitement when he spoke about his unborn child.

"I'm sure he will, but then he'll have an older cousin to play with him."

"Very true."

The men followed Peter inside and to the kitchen where Erica was getting Peter a snack. She glanced at them and smiled, giving Cole an extra look of curiosity before turning her full attention to Peter.

She listened as he told her about one of his classes. Then, when he focused on his snack, he fell silent.

Erica put a hand on his shoulder. "I'm going to be right out here talking to Uncle Bryce and Mr. Shepherd. Why don't you eat your snack and take a thirty-minute break before tackling your homework?"

"Okay," he said through a mouth full of chips.

The three adults stepped into the living room area. Erica gave her brother a hug. "Thanks for picking him up for me."

"You know it's never a problem." Bryce tweaked her nose, and she batted at his hand with a chuckle.

Cole smiled as he watched them.

Erica turned to him then, her face becoming more serious. "Did you find Bethany?"

"I did not." He told her how he'd checked with professors at the community college, but no one had seen her today. "So, according to her roommate, Bethany left their house this morning like she normally did. Except, to our knowledge, she wasn't seen after that."

"I don't like this. I know I'm probably nervous after everything else that's happened this week, but I sure would feel better if we knew Bethany was okay."

Cole hated that she was so worried. He also had a bad feeling about all of it. Coincidences certainly happened, but the mess surrounding Erica right now seemed to be much more than that.

His phone rang, and Asher's name flashed on the screen.

"Please excuse me. I need to take this." He walked into the dining room before answering the call. "Hey, Asher. What have you got?"

"I ran a background check on Rumford like you requested. Talk about a really interesting guy. He's been investigated multiple times for embezzlement and none of the allegations have ever stuck. He *is* in town for a business conference, but I'm not sure why he's attending. The conference is all about customer service and relations. He doesn't work in that area at all." There were some shuffling noises in the background. "I'm not even sure he deals with customers. He's more like a gopher for the vice president of his company."

"That's interesting. Is he married?"

"Never married. No kids that I could find."

"Maybe he's having an affair with someone at the conference? But if he were, he wouldn't be coming back to the B&B every evening. He'd either be bringing a lady friend, or he'd be out late." Cole thought back over the last few days and his interactions with Rumford. The guy seemed normal. Boring, even.

"I can dig into the conference a little. See if there's anyone else attending from Rumford's hometown."

"I appreciate the offer, Asher. I started wondering last night if someone might have been casing the B&B for him instead of Erica. But it doesn't add up. Why go after Erica if that's the case?"

"I tend to agree. The guy seems a bit shady, but I don't think he's connected. Is there anyone else you want me to look into?"

"Bethany Massy." He gave Asher her address and everything else he knew about her. "We haven't been able to locate her today. Could be nothing, but the timing is suspicious. At this point, I'm willing to investigate anything that's a little odd."

"Will do."

Cole ended the call. He could still see Erica and Bryce talking in the other room. The instinct to protect her was so strong that he questioned it. Clearly, she had a brother and a whole community who were there for her, so why did the idea of not watching out for her bother him so much?

"What do you want me to do?" he whispered the prayer.

He thought about the way she'd been forced off the road. If he hadn't been there, would the SUV have doubled back? Would Erica and Peter be the ones missing now?

Chapter Nine

When Erica woke up Thursday morning, the first thought that crossed her mind was Bethany. It had taken a while to fall asleep last night. Between Bethany's disappearance and everything else that had happened in the last week, Erica was exhausted. With a sigh, she got out of bed, made it, and headed for the shower.

After making sure Peter was up and going, she went to the dining room to get breakfast set up. Peter came down not long later, extra energy in his step. Erica immediately knew why.

"Football practice is tonight!" he announced, excitement lacing his voice.

It was sometimes hard for Erica to believe how much her son loved the sport at his age. It was ironic because she hadn't been the least interested in football or the players when she was in high school. In fact, she didn't go to a single football game until Peter started playing.

"That means you'd better eat a good breakfast to start your day off right," she told him with a smile.

Cole walked into the room then, and Peter wasted no time telling him about his football practice. "You should come and watch, Mr. Shepherd. It's a lot of fun!" With that, he ran off to choose his breakfast.

"Peter has loved football since he was old enough to say the word. I signed him up with the league as soon as he turned seven," Erica told Cole with a chuckle. "It's quite entertaining to watch at times."

"I can imagine." He smiled after Peter, but it quickly disappeared, replaced by a look of concern. "I just heard from Bethany's roommate, Lynn. Bethany never came home last night. She's going down to the police station to file a missing person's report."

Erica pressed a hand to her mouth. She kept hoping that Bethany would turn up. That she'd call and apologize for not coming in to work. But deep down, Erica knew something must have happened. "I hope the police can find her. I'm praying that's the case, but I have a horrible feeling..." She stopped. It was better not to voice these things out loud. Not now, certainly.

"I know." Cole reached out and gently squeezed her hand.

A pulse of awareness went straight to her heart. He released it again, the cool air rushing in to replace the warmth of his palm.

"Do you need someone to take Peter to school?" he asked.

"Bryce said he'd pick him up and take him. Thank you, though. Mr. Rumford will be checking out this morning, so I mostly need to make sure I'm here until after that. What are your plans for the day?" She led the way to the dining area and poured two cups of coffee.

He took his with a nod of thanks, his fingers brushing

against hers. "I'll be waiting to hear from the realtor some-time this morning. The Durhams made an offer on the place, and the realtor thought they would have an answer sooner rather than later. I'm hoping to get all of that sorted out before the end of the day."

Which meant he wouldn't have to stay in Destiny after that. The thought of him leaving made her sad. Which was silly. She'd only met him a few days ago.

"Well, I hope everything comes together the way you all want it to. If so, are you planning to check out this evening or tomorrow?"

"I'm not sure. Maybe I'll stick around for a few more days." He shrugged as though it were no big deal, but there was something in his eyes that made her question his reasons.

Whatever they were, Erica would be happy to have him around longer. She had no guest reservations for the week-end, which meant she and Peter would be in the large building by themselves. It happened frequently, and with everything that had happened recently, she didn't look forward to it. Having Cole around made her feel a little better.

"You're welcome to stay for as long as you'd like."

He held her gaze for several heartbeats. "I appreciate that."

Peter ran past them and into the kitchen.

Cole glanced at him, and when he looked back at her, his expression had grown serious. "I have a question for you."

Erica paused. Her mind raced as she tried to figure out what he wanted to ask her. "What is it?"

"Would you mind if I tagged along to football practice tonight? Peter made it sound like I shouldn't miss it. I figure it'd be a shame to pass up the opportunity to watch a bunch of rambunctious boys play football." The seriousness on his face morphed into a grin. He slipped his hands into his pockets.

She laughed, thankful for something to ease the tension of the morning. "You're more than welcome to. I know Peter will be thrilled, but don't say I didn't warn you about the chaos."

Cole stayed busy all morning and never had to leave the B&B. He got a text early from Asher who'd done a thorough search on Bethany but turned up nothing unusual. Cole wasn't surprised, but he was disappointed that the search hadn't resulted in a lead of some kind.

The realtor contacted him, and the owner of the boys' home accepted Greg's offer. She dropped by with paper-work for Cole to take back home, but Greg and Ruth would eventually have to travel to Destiny to sign everything when it was time for closing. For now, getting inspections done would be one of the first steps.

Erica seemed to stay busy, too. Once Rumford checked out, she came up to his old room. He heard her bumping around and was just about to walk over to ask her about lunch when she walked out with an armful of linens.

He held onto both of her arms to make sure she didn't trip. "Sorry about that."

"No problem." She lowered the basket full of sheets so she could see him better. "Obviously I wasn't watching where I was going."

He dropped his hands. "It's almost noon. I was thinking

of trying a place the realtor recommended. The Corner Café. She said they serve great hamburgers."

"Yes, they do. And their cinnamon rolls are out of this world, too."

"If I ran by and picked up a couple of burgers and some fries and brought them back here, would you be interested in joining me for lunch?" Cole shouldn't care, but he really hoped she'd say yes. Being able to just relax a little with her would be awesome.

"I'd like that," she said with a tip of her chin and a pretty smile on her face. "Thank you."

"In that case, I'll be back in a little while. Can I carry that down to the utility room for you?"

"No, I've got it. Thank you. I'll see you in a bit."

Since he got to The Corner Café right in the middle of the lunch rush, it took some time for them to get his order ready.

The aroma from his to-go bag filled the cab of his truck to the point where he had to reach over for a fry. It tasted even better than it looked.

Back at the B&B, he walked into the main room to find Erica talking on her cell phone. He froze, wondering if it was news about Bethany.

"Of course, Bryce. It'll be fine." She looked up, saw Cole, and gave him a smile.

He relaxed a little and went to the kitchen to set the food down.

Erica followed him. "I hope Megan feels better. If you guys need anything, let me know. I can bring groceries by or pick up some chicken noodle soup. Just say the word." She grabbed some napkins as she listened to Bryce talk. "I will. Love you, too. Give Megan a hug for me." She hung up and set the phone down on the table.

"Everything okay?"

"Megan's got a cold. At least we're hoping it's just a cold and not something worse. Poor thing, being sick while pregnant is miserable. Anyway, he wanted to let me know. They usually go to Peter's football games on Saturdays, and then we often have lunch together on Sundays. But he doesn't want us to get sick, too." She retrieved plates from one of the cabinets and set them on the table along with the napkins.

"Definitely understandable." He began to unpack the bags. "I hope Megan recovers quickly and that Bryce avoids getting sick at all."

"I appreciate that." She got condiments from the fridge. "Thank you for lunch. It smells fantastic. I didn't realize how hungry I was until you came in with all of this."

They got something to drink and sat down to eat.

Cole took a large bite of his burger and nodded appreciatively. It lived up to the hype. "So when and where is Peter's game this weekend?"

"It's in Fredericksburg at five in the evening." She'd started to reach for a fry but stopped. The smile that was on her face a moment ago disappeared.

"What is it?"

"With Bethany missing, maybe we should stay in town and skip the game. It seems wrong to go to football games and have fun and laugh when we don't know what she might be going through right now..." Her voice caught.

"Trust me, I get that. But there's little you can do right now. Make sure your phone is on, and Fredericksburg isn't so far away that you can't head back immediately if something comes up. It'll probably be good for you—and Peter—to have something else to focus on for a few hours."

She seemed to think about that and finally nodded. "Yeah. I know you're right. I do with the game was earlier in the day, though. With it starting at five o'clock, it'll be relatively late by the time we get home because the team goes out for dinner afterward."

"Do Bryce and Megan usually go to all of his games?" He picked up a fry and popped it into his mouth.

"Someone does, especially when it's an away game. If Megan is working or Bryce is on shift, my parents will go. They're on vacation right now. They decided to travel across the states along Route 66 for their anniversary." She smiled, her blue eyes sparkling. "They figured it was a good time to go since Megan isn't due for another two months."

"What a neat trip idea." Going on an extended road trip like that sounded great. There were a lot of places in the United States he hadn't seen that were on his bucket list. "So then you and Peter will be going to Fredericksburg alone on Saturday?" He tried to make the question casual, but the idea of them driving that distance without someone to watch their backs bothered him.

"Yes. I prefer the mid-day games because then we can get home again well before it starts to get dark. There are a lot of deer between here and there."

"I can imagine." He wanted to offer to go with them but didn't know how she'd feel about it. It was one thing to go to the practice tonight and drive his own vehicle. It was a whole different situation to invite himself along on Saturday. So he held his tongue and took another bite of his lunch. "It's nice your family is so close."

"It is. I'm thankful for all of them. I don't know how I would've done it without them, especially during Peter's early years. It's too bad my parents are out of town. I'd have liked for you to meet them." The moment the words were out of her mouth, pink climbed her neck and traveled to her cheeks. "I just mean they normally would've been by the B&B by now, so you would've met them naturally."

She got up and refilled her glass of water that was still half full.

Cole fought back a smile. He knew what she'd meant, although the slip-up—and her resulting embarrassment—were cute. "It is too bad that it didn't work out."

Erica reached into the small cooler at her feet and took out two bottles of water, handing one of them to Cole. He accepted it with a thanks. She'd learned early on never to go to a football practice or game without a cooler full of water, Gatorade, and a few snacks.

They were sitting in the stands watching Peter and his team practice. She tried to ignore the sweat that ran in rivulets down her back. As much as she looked forward to cooler football practices and games, she tried to remind herself how miserable it could be to sit outside in the cold weather later.

Twice, Peter looked up at the stands from the field and waved. Erica was certain Peter realized and appreciated that she went to every single one of his games and practices, but she wasn't going to fool herself into thinking the waves were for her.

When Peter found out that Cole was going to be here, the boy was so excited. She couldn't blame him. It was definitely nice not to be sitting up here alone.

Cole rested his elbows on his knees as he watched the field. "You're right. This is entertaining. Those boys sure do give it their all, don't they?"

"Yes, they do." She pointed out Peter's friend, Shawn,

who was also on the team. "Those two are practically inseparable."

"It's important to have a friend like that growing up."

"Yes, it is." She glanced at Cole's profile. There was something about the tone of his voice that suggested he might not have had the same luxury. "Obviously, I can't control everything. But I'm hoping and praying for a group of friends—good kids—who can grow up together."

"Are you speaking from experience?" He turned to look at her.

"From the perspective of not having that kind of support group. I connected with the wrong crowd and got into a lot of trouble. Especially in high school." She wrinkled her nose. There were a lot of things she did back then that she wasn't proud of. "I met my ex during our senior year. My parents, and even Bryce, warned me Jeffery was no good, but that made me gravitate toward him even more. They were right, of course, but I didn't find out until we'd been married two years, and Peter was on the way."

"I'm sorry to hear that." He braced his left hand on the stadium bench and angled his body toward her. "Although I'm having a hard time picturing you as anything remotely close to a delinquent."

"I'm glad to hear my years of hard work and reformation have paid off." She grinned at him.

He gave a hearty laugh, and his upper arm brushed against hers when he shifted to face forward again. Erica didn't move away.

A moment later, a sudden sadness filled her heart and caused tears to build. She sniffed and tried to subtly wipe them away, but Cole noticed immediately.

"What's wrong? The game's not that bad." He flashed a teasing smile, but his eyes held concern.

She chuckled at his joke, but the humor didn't last. "I was thinking about Bethany. She always asks Peter how his practice went the next day..."

They watched the practice in heavy silence for a while. Erica's gaze wandered to the sideline, where the coach was talking to one of the kids. She scanned the seats until her attention caught on a man standing at the far end where other parents were gathered.

Recognition hit her like a blow to the gut, and she gasped. The granola bar she was eating fell from her hand and landed on the concrete by her feet.

"Erica?"

Her heart thudded in her chest as the sound of her own pulse echoed in her ears.

"Erica? What's wrong?"

She jumped when Cole put a hand on her arm. "That man. Down there in the navy long-sleeved shirt and a baseball cap at the end." She pointed to him. "I think that's the guy who was in the passenger seat of the SUV that ran us off the road."

Chapter Ten

Cole tensed as he followed Erica's gaze to the man she was pointing out. "Are you sure?" Not that he doubted her. But there were a lot of people out here in baseball caps, and this guy was pretty far away.

The man looked in their direction and stalled. If Cole had any reservation about it before, it was gone now. The man clearly recognized Erica.

Cole was tempted to jump up and run after him, but the distance between them would make it nearly impossible to catch him. Instead, he pulled out his phone and opened the camera app. He zoomed in before lifting it up and taking a picture.

Their suspect's eyes widened. He casually turned and walked away from the crowd toward the parking lot beyond.

"Stay here." Cole squeezed Erica's hand. "I'm going to follow him and try to get a license plate number from whatever vehicle he's driving." He went to release her hand, but she tightened her grip.

"Be careful." The concern in her eyes, accentuated by a hint of fear, touched his heart.

"I will."

She released his hand, and he weaved his way through the spectators until he was at the edge of the small crowd. The suspect continued to walk at a steady but fast pace through the parking lot.

Cole had his phone out so he could snap a picture of the vehicle and, with any luck, the license plate number. But between the suspect's head start and the influx of cars for the next set of practices, all Cole could see was that it was a navy blue, mid-size car. He thought it was a Nissan Altima but wasn't a hundred percent sure.

He called Asher, who picked up on the second ring. "Hey, man. We saw the passenger from the SUV that ran Erica and Peter off the road. I'm going to send you a picture. I'm hoping you can enhance it and run it through facial recognition, but I have my doubts." Then he relayed the car information while he waited for the picture to go through. "I know it's not a lot to work with, but it's more than we had ten minutes ago."

"Got the photo. I'll see what I can do."

"I appreciate it." Cole scanned the stands until he located Erica. Happy to see that she was still there and safe, he made his way back and sat down beside her.

"I'm glad you're back," she said. "Any luck?"

He pulled the photo up and showed it to her.

Unfortunately, it wasn't even as clear as he'd hoped it would be. But apparently it was enough because Erica immediately nodded. "It's definitely him. The logo on the hat—he wore the same one in the SUV." It wasn't cold, but she crossed her arms in front of her and rubbed at the goose-bumps that had formed along them. "Did he follow us here? And if so, why?"

Cole put an arm around her, hoping to offer her a little

warmth and comfort. "I don't know. But the way he took off once you spotted him tells me he was trying to stay discreet. I get the impression he was watching you rather than waiting for the opportunity to interact with you."

The whole thing made Cole uneasy.

When Erica leaned into his shoulder, Cole decided to leave his arm around hers. She texted Jenny the information, and then they watched the rest of practice, both of them keeping a close eye on Peter and the crowd of people around the field. When it was over, Cole dropped his arm, and Erica stood and stretched.

She had a Gatorade and a container of peanut butter crackers out and waiting when Peter ran up. His forehead glistened with sweat, and a smile lit up his face. "Did you see me, Mom? Did you see that tackle?"

"I sure did, honey." She twisted the top off the drink and handed it to him. "You guys worked hard out there today."

He nodded emphatically. "Sure did. Really hard." He popped a peanut butter cracker into his mouth, barely chewed it up, and swallowed before stating, "I'm starving!"

"Get your gear together, and we'll head out." Erica replaced the cap on his drink and set it back in the cooler. She looked at Cole and wrinkled her nose. "I apologize for the smell in the car. Boys and sports."

Cole gave a hearty laugh. "If you think it's bad now, wait until he's a teenager. You'll probably have to drive home with the windows down."

She looked disgusted, but there was a twinkle of humor in her eyes. "That sounds like something to look forward to."

"Hey, before Peter gets back, I wanted to offer to order a pizza when we get back to the B&B. I just didn't want to say anything in front of him in case there's a reason why you would prefer I didn't." He'd considered offering to take them both out somewhere for dinner, but he didn't know if Peter had brought a full change of clothes with him. He didn't want to come off as too forward with Erica, either.

"Oh, you don't have to do that."

"And if I'd like to?"

The corners of her mouth lifted. "Then I think that would be wonderful, thank you."

"Anytime." Their gazes tangled for several moments until Peter ran back to them, his duffel bag over one shoulder. Erica was the first to look away, but Cole didn't miss the blush that worked its way into her cheeks.

What was going on with him when it came to Erica? He knew full well even *considering* a relationship was a bad idea, especially when it came with a ready-made family. He was going to be leaving soon... and maybe not moving to Destiny at all. He had no right to flirt with Erica or try to spend more time with her.

Except that he couldn't help himself. There was something about her that pulled him in like gravity.

By the time they pulled up to the B&B, Erica was thankful that Cole had offered to order pizza. She was drained, both emotionally and physically. She kept glancing in the rearview mirror all the way back, half expecting to see either the SUV or this new navy blue car driving behind them. Of course, there was nothing to worry about.

The second she put the car in park and turned off the ignition, Peter flung his door open and got out. "I can't wait for pizza!"

"Well, you need to take a shower first," she reminded him. "And let's make it quick so you'll be all done before the pizza arrives." She shot Cole a smile and got out of the car herself. With keys in hand, she glanced up at the second floor just in time to see the curtains in one of the windows slide back into place.

Her heart jumped to her throat, and she snagged Peter's arm before he took off for the front door.

"Cole! There's someone inside on the second floor."

His gaze pinged from her to the windows. "You and Peter get back into the car and call the police. Lock the doors." He reached over and took the keys from her hand.

"What are you going to do?" She panicked at the thought of him going inside and possibly facing whoever was in there.

"I'm going to see what's going on." He pulled a handgun from his waistband. "Stay here. I'll be back in a minute."

Erica wanted to object but couldn't form the words fast enough to stop him. He was at the front door and inside in a blink. Worry gnawed at her stomach as she dialed the all-too-familiar number for the police department and reported the situation. Someone she didn't know assured her the police were on the way.

She opened the app to see if any of the cameras had caught the intruder. Not surprisingly, the Wi-Fi was out again, which only convinced Erica further that someone was inside, and it was the same person who had been prowling around the B&B before.

She kept waiting for Cole to come back out of the house, but he didn't until the sirens sounded as they came down the street. When she finally saw him again, and he appeared to be fine, she relaxed enough to lean into her seat. The instinct to run over and give him a hug surprised her.

"Peter, I need you to stay here for a few more minutes, please. I'm going to talk to Mr. Shepherd and the police and make sure it's okay for us to go inside."

"Okay." The poor kid's voice sounded uncertain. "You promise you'll be right here?"

"I won't leave your sight." She reached back and patted his knee before getting out of the car.

Officer Clint Baker was there, and so were Officer Gabe Harrison and his K-9 partner, Loki. They all met Cole in front of the house.

"The front door was unlocked when I tested it." Cole glanced at Erica. "But I remember watching Erica lock it before we left a couple of hours ago."

"When we pulled up, I saw someone in one of the upstairs windows. It should be the first room on the left once you get up there." She suppressed a shiver. What was the intruder doing in her B&B? Her home? She pictured all kinds of damage or items stolen, and her fear morphed into anger.

"When was the last time you rented that particular room out?" Gabe asked.

"It's been a couple of weeks."

"Perfect. Loki should be able to get a clear scent then." He offered her a comforting smile. "We're going to get to the bottom of this."

"I appreciate it."

Clint withdrew his gun. "We'll be back after we clear the building."

With that, the two officers and Loki went inside.

Cole holstered his own weapon before placing a hand against her lower back and guiding her to the car. "Let's move away from the door. I didn't hear anyone inside, but if they flush someone out, we don't want to be in the way."

She hadn't thought about that and hurried back to the car and Peter. She opened a back door so she could speak to him. "It'll be just a few more minutes."

Peter didn't look convinced. "Mom? Why are people messing with us?"

Erica's heart ached at the worry on his face. She motioned for him to come out of the car and pulled him into a hug. "I don't know, honey. Sometimes people get so angry that they take it out on others, which isn't right or fair. Hopefully the police can catch whoever keeps doing these things and can get him help so he won't be as angry anymore."

Cole knelt on the ground so that he was at eye-level with Peter. "And I'm going to do everything I can to keep you and your mom safe. Okay?"

Peter nodded. "Okay." His attention went to the B&B and then back to Cole. "Can we still order pizza?"

Her son's innocent question followed by Cole's deep laugh was the light Erica needed. She smiled at them both.

"Of course we can, buddy. We'll order two pizzas, then we'll have enough leftovers for tomorrow. How does that sound?"

"Yes!" Peter did a fist pump.

Erica had Peter get back in the car when, after what felt like an hour, Clint and Gabe came around the outside of the B&B from the back door.

She crossed her arms tightly in front of her and waited for the report.

"There was no evidence that anyone had been in the house when they weren't supposed to be," Clint began. "That said, the front door was unlocked as reported. The interesting thing is that the backdoor was locked, but only the lock on the doorknob. The deadbolt wasn't secured. Do you usually leave that deadbolt in place when you're gone?"

"Absolutely. I usually leave it locked even when we're here. We don't go out that way very often." Does that mean someone had locked the door on the way out? Talk about unusual.

Gabe tossed Loki a ball and gave him a hearty ear scratch. "Loki caught a scent in the room you told us about. He followed it downstairs to your apartment area and the entrance and finally to the backdoor. From there, we tracked the scent through the property behind yours. It went cold at the road."

"The suspect likely got into a vehicle from there and drove away," Clint added.

Erica held up her phone. "I checked when we first got here, and the Wi-Fi was out again, so nothing was caught on the cameras." She checked the app again to find everything was up and running. "Which makes me think that this is the same person who was lurking outside the other night."

"May I see it?" Clint held out a hand and checked the logs as well. "It sure seems that way." He frowned. "We saw no sign of forced entry. It looks like someone walked right in. Who all has keys? Or access to keys?"

"My parents have a set. My dad keeps them on his keyring, and they're on vacation out of state. I gave a set to Bryce and Megan." Erica stopped as a thought hit her. Waves of realization were quickly followed by sadness. "Bethany has a set, too." Her voice trailed off.

Had these people done something to Bethany for a set of keys to gain access to the house? If so, why? None of this made sense. She squeezed her eyes shut against the possibilities swirling in her mind.

"Hey. Erica." Cole's voice brought her attention to him.

She opened her eyes to find him standing in front of her, his hands on her shoulders. "We don't know anything for sure. Dwelling on uncertain possibilities only takes your attention from what we need to deal with now. Focus on Peter. On the problem that's right in front of us. Then we take it one step at a time."

Chapter Eleven

Officer Baker took Erica inside the B&B so they could walk through it, room by room, and see if anything was missing. Meanwhile, Officer Harrison called Peter over to play fetch with Loki, giving Harrison and Cole a few minutes to talk.

"Have you guys made any headway on locating Bethany?" As much as he had wanted to help Erica focus on something else, he'd had the same thoughts. Bethany going missing when she did was no coincidence. He just prayed they were all wrong, and the poor woman would turn up somewhere soon.

"Nothing. It's like she vanished." Harrison frowned. "Just like the SUV and the man who broke in this evening. We might as well be chasing a shadow."

"But they *will* make a mistake eventually. And we'll be there when they do." Of that, Cole was certain. He hoped it would be sooner than later. "Did Officer Durant tell you about the guy we saw at the football game?"

"No, I haven't spoken to her."

Cole told him about the man that Erica recognized. "At

the time, we were trying to figure out why he was there. Now I'm wondering if he was keeping an eye on us to verify that we were at the game and letting his partner know that the coast was clear at the B&B."

"It certainly tracks. If the guy tonight was the same person who was in the passenger seat in the SUV, and then the lookout tonight. I'd say the other guy, whoever he is, must be the boss." He watched Peter and Loki play for a few moments, a small smile on his face. But the smile faded as quickly as it appeared. "We need to get the locks changed immediately. I know someone who could probably head over here and get right to work."

While Harrison reached out to his source, Cole called for pizza delivery. He'd made a promise to Peter, and he intended to keep it.

Peter tossed the ball to Loki again, but instead of bringing it back this time, dog laid down on the ground beside Harrison and started to chew on the ball.

Peter walked over to stand next to Cole. "I wish I had a dog. One day, when I can get one, I want a German shepherd just like Loki."

"They do make great pets," Harrison said after ending his call. "But they also have a lot of energy and need a lot of attention and time to play. Make sure you remember that when the time comes."

"Yes, sir, I will." His voice was so serious that both men had to fight to keep smiles from their faces.

Forty-five minutes later, Peter was eating pizza and watching a movie on the TV in the main room. The officers had left, but a locksmith was still there replacing all the locks.

Erica spent most of the time on the phone—first with her brother and then with her parents. Cole heard her reassure them that they didn't need to come home early. When she hung up, she noticed him nearby.

"They've never gone on a trip like this. The last thing they need to do is call it off just to come home to this mess." She shrugged before walking over to the coffee table where two boxes of pizza rested. She chose a slice of pepperoni and took a bite. "I had no idea how badly I needed this."

Cole's stomach growled, pushing him to grab a slice of sausage and nod his agreement. It'd been a long evening.

By the time the locksmith finished, it was nearing nine. Peter was starting to yawn, and even Erica looked exhausted. The skin below her eyes had darkened from lack of sleep and worry.

She double- and triple-checked that both doors were locked before excusing herself and Peter. They went to their apartment to get him ready for bed.

Cole cleaned up the pizza and paper plates then poured himself another cup of coffee. If protecting Erica and her son was a job he'd been hired for, he would have requested backup—someone to take turns with him staying alert all night. There shouldn't be a need for it now that the locks had been changed, but he had a feeling it would make Erica feel better.

He offered her a cup of coffee, which she readily accepted before going back to the living area and collapsing on the couch. "What. A. Day." She took a sip and closed her eyes, her head resting against the back of the couch. "Thanks again for the pizza. And for coming with us to football practice."

"It's not a problem at all." He set his mug on the coffee table. Thinking she might need a distraction, he told her about Peter playing with Loki.

She opened her eyes, a smile on her face. "He wants a

dog so badly." She took another drink and set her mug down, too. "To be honest, lately I've been thinking about selling this place."

That surprised him. Owning a business like this was a big accomplishment. She seemed like such a natural at it. "It's clear you've put a lot of time and effort into this place. Why would you want to sell it?"

"I'd like to own an actual house. One with a fenced-in yard so Peter could have a dog. I mean, every boy should grow up with a dog." There was a sad tone to her voice. "It'd be nice not to have to share the house with strangers. I don't really mind it, but when we have guests, I'm on duty day and night. I'd like to go to work and then, at the end of my shift, go home. You know?"

"That makes perfect sense, Erica. I don't blame you. I'm sure this can be a lot sometimes." Especially this last week. If she hadn't been considering selling the place before, he wouldn't have blamed her for thinking about it now. "How's your sister-in-law feeling?"

Erica reached for her mug again. "She sounds awful. I feel so bad for her. I think she's going to go in and see the doctor tomorrow. Hopefully they can suggest something to help her with the cough that's safe to take while pregnant."

"I hope she improves soon."

"Thank you. Bryce had a scratchy throat, too. I'm sad they'll miss Peter's game tomorrow, but I'm glad they won't be sharing germs."

They talked about the football practice and what it was like to watch a bunch of elementary school kids out on the field.

By the time they finished their coffee, it was well after ten, and Erica was constantly covering a yawn.

"I guess I should go try to get some sleep." She rubbed

her palms on the legs of her pants and then crossed her arms tightly in front of her. "It's just that every time I close my eyes, I picture Bethany's face. I can't stop wondering where she is. Is she hurt or scared? Or worse..." Her voice caught.

"The not knowing is horrible." He'd had to push similar thoughts from his mind as well, and he barely knew Bethany. The very idea that someone might be harming her made him angry. "We'll keep praying the police make some headway soon."

"I know it's really all we can do." Erica sighed and ran a hand through her hair in frustration. "But it doesn't seem like nearly enough."

"No, it doesn't."

Silence descended on the room. Finally, Erica stood with a sigh.

Cole got to his feet and cleared his throat. "I had an idea, and I thought I'd run it past you." He truly had no idea what her reaction was going to be. "With everything that's happening, I'd feel better if I were down here tonight. Do you have any objection to my sleeping on the couch?"

Erica's eyes widened. Clearly, she hadn't anticipated the request. "I'd hate for you to do that. I mean, you're paying for a room. There's no way that couch will be nearly as comfortable." She frowned. "After everything that's happened, I wouldn't blame you if you wanted to check out tomorrow. I should give you a refund for at least one night."

"Hey." He reached over and covered her hand with his. "That's not what I meant at all. I don't want a refund. I'm choosing to stay. And if you have no objections, I'm choosing to sleep down here on the couch. Trust me. I'll rest better being on the same floor as you and Peter."

He hadn't meant to say it quite like that. It was true,

though. It would be better to be close by in case they had any issues tonight.

He thought she was going to object again. Instead, her gaze went to their hands, and he could see her visibly relax. "If you're sure, I'd feel better knowing someone else was down here too." Her chin lifted then, and her blue eyes fixed on his face.

It took everything in Cole not to lean in and kiss her. The moment he made that decision, he regretted it. But there was a reason why he'd always been determined to stay single. How did this beautiful woman manage to keep getting under his skin?

Erica almost turned her hand over. She had a feeling that holding hands with him would feel natural. Right.

Then he'd looked at her, and something in his eyes made her breath catch. She desperately wanted him to kiss her. But to what end? He was going to be leaving in another day or two, and the last thing Peter needed in his life was instability.

She slid her hand out and stood. "Let me get a pillow and some blankets for you. The least we can do is make sure you're as comfortable as possible."

She grabbed their empty mugs and deposited them in the kitchen sink before heading to the linen closet upstairs. Ten minutes later, she had the couch made up. "Is there anything else you need?"

"Are you kidding? I may be sleeping on the couch, but I think I have more here than I would at most hotels." He gave her a smile. "Thank you for your hospitality. I appreciate it."

"No, thank *you*. I don't know how I would have made it through the last few days without your help." When she realized what she said, warmth flooded her cheeks. "Good night, Cole."

Erica retreated to her apartment and got ready for bed. She dreaded trying to sleep and still felt uneasy when she checked on Peter. Seeing her son's peaceful face eased her worry a little. After straightening his blanket, she whispered a prayer. "Dear heavenly Father. Thank You for watching over us today and for keeping us safe." She prayed for Megan to feel better, for her parents' safety as they traveled... and for Bethany. Then she ended with, "Please help Peter, Cole, and me to get some rest tonight. We all need it desperately. In Your Son's name I pray, amen."

She watched Peter's chest rise and fall several more times before leaving the room. When she went to bed herself, she fell into blissful slumber the moment her head hit the pillow.

The next thing she knew, it was Friday morning, and her alarm was going off. Not only had she not had nightmares, but apparently neither had Peter. Her eyes still felt heavy, but she noticed a lack of soreness as she got out of bed. It was so nice not to hurt every time she moved.

Back in the dining room, she found Cole had already started the coffee machine. When he saw her, he greeted her with a smile and a steaming mug.

"Thank you." She took a sip and released a happy sigh. "Did you get any sleep last night?"

"Honestly? I slept much better than I thought I would. How about you and Peter?"

"Same. Thank you again for camping downstairs. I'm pretty sure that was a big factor." Knowing that he was here, and that no one could sneak into the building, had been very comforting.

"What's on your to-do list for the day?"

"I need to take Peter to school, then get some paperwork done around here for a while. Around lunch, I want to swing by a deli in town and pick up some chicken noodle soup to drop off for Bryce and Megan. I have some things to get at the church too." She shrugged. "Fridays are usually my day to get caught up and do some of the random things I haven't gotten around to all week." Mostly cleaning, preparing rooms for guests who might be checking in over the weekend, and grocery runs when needed. With no reservations in the books and only Cole as a guest, there was a lot less to do.

Cole scratched his trimmed goatee and studied her for a moment or two. "Would you like some company?"

"I appreciate the offer, Cole. But you shouldn't feel obligated to be my unofficial bodyguard. You've already gone above and beyond. Seriously, if you sent me a bill, I wouldn't blame you."

He laughed and shook his head. "I don't feel obligated. I want to make sure my new friend is safe, and there's always more safety in numbers." He shrugged. "Besides, getting the chance to get to know you better and see more of Destiny wouldn't be a bad thing."

There was no mistaking the interest in his eyes, and it had her heart tumbling in her chest. She ought to tell him no. Especially when spending time together would only strengthen her attraction to him—something she needed to avoid, considering he was going to be leaving soon.

On the other hand, having someone there with her today would go a long way in making her feel more comfortable. And that would be true if it were Bryce or Jenny or anyone else. She didn't particularly want to be alone today.

Cole must have been able to sense her tumultuous thoughts. "I tend to speak my mind, and sometimes that's a little much. I apologize if I made you uncomfortable. You won't hurt my feelings if you say no."

"It's not that. I'd love to hang out with my new friend, too. Thanks for offering."

"Thank you for accepting." He smiled.

Peter came downstairs then. "I'm starving! Hi, Mr. Shepherd."

"Good morning, Peter. Did you sleep well?"

"Sure did." His gaze went to the breakfast bar, but he stopped and faced Cole. "How long are you going to stay? If you're here tomorrow, you should come to my football game!"

"Peter," Erica chided, "it's an away game." She made a mental note to talk to him about when it is and isn't appropriate to invite people.

The boy cringed. "I forgot. Sorry, Mr. Shepherd. Maybe next time you come to town, I'll have a game here at home."

With that, he ran off to get some breakfast.

Cole stifled a smile. "I'm going to head upstairs and get ready. See you in a bit?"

Less than an hour later, they were on the road again. Erica drove this time, and while she found herself checking the rearview mirror frequently, she wasn't quite as on edge as she had been. She took that as a sign that, at some point, she wouldn't worry about someone trying to run her off the road.

Cole's phone pinged with a text. He read it and then turned the phone off again. "Asher couldn't get any hits off the photo I took. He said it wasn't clear enough for the computer to do a thorough search."

Disappointment washed over Erica, although she wasn't surprised by the results. It'd been worth a shot, though.

They got Peter dropped off at school and headed for Destiny Church of the Nazarene. She parked along the curb in front of the main entrance. "I have a room upstairs at the B&B where I organize and store clothing donations that come in to the church so it's easy to find things when we need them." She led the way through the door and to the right. "Penny texted me yesterday to let me know there were two bags waiting."

They used a small closet in the children's wing to store clothing until there was enough for Erica to pick it up. On the way by the office, she stuck her head in and let Penny know they were there. Penny was on the phone, but her face brightened as she waved her greeting.

Erica and Cole each grabbed a garbage bag full of clothing and made their way back to the front of the church. Penny was still on the phone, so Erica decided to text her goodbye rather than interrupt her.

They got the clothing loaded, and Erica was maneuvering the car through the parking lot when her cell phone rang. She glanced at the screen. The Destiny Police Department popped up on the caller ID.

She pulled into a spot near the parking lot exit and swiped to answer it. "Hello?"

"Erica, it's Jenny." Her tone was too even. "We found Bethany's car."

Erica wanted to be hopeful, but she could tell by Jenny's voice that the news wasn't good. "And Bethany?"

"I'm so sorry, Erica. She's dead."

Chapter Twelve

When Erica's shoulders dropped and she scrambled to get out of the car, Cole knew the news wasn't good. He got out as well but stayed on his side of the car to give her some space. He thought the call might have ended until she spoke again, her voice quiet.

"No, it's fine. Of course. We'll be there soon." Her arms fell to her sides, and she leaned against the car.

When she didn't move, Cole rounded the vehicle to find her face stricken.

She lifted her gaze to him, her eyes brimming with tears. "Bethany's gone." The words were barely above a whisper. "Why are these guys after me? Is it my fault she's dead?"

She leaned forward then, and he wrapped her in his arms as she cried, her cheek pressed against his chest as silent sobs wracked her body.

Cole's heart tore over her pain. He said nothing—because there were no words to ease her torment right now. All he could do was hold her, let her know she wasn't alone, and pray that God would cover her with the kind of peace that only He possessed.

He wasn't sure how long they stood there, but when her crying subsided, and she stepped back, he pulled out a handkerchief and handed it to her. She nodded her thanks and used it to dry her eyes and blow her nose.

She finally raised her head and squared her shoulders.

Erica Keyes was a fighter, and Cole respected her all the more for it.

"This is *not* your fault." His voice was firm, and he held eye contact. "The guys responsible for this are cowards, and everything that has happened rests entirely on their shoulders. We're going to figure out who they are, and they will be held accountable for what they've done to Bethany. For what they've done to you and Peter. Do you understand me?"

Erica nodded and sniffed as one last tear escaped from the corner of her eye and rolled down her cheek.

Cole reached over and gently brushed it away with the pad of his thumb. He was tempted to pull her in for another hug. Instead, he placed a hand against her back. "Come on, I'll drive us to the police department."

When they arrived, Officer Durant gave Erica a comforting hug and led them to a conference room where Officer Baker was waiting. They all sat down. Before they began, another man Cole didn't recognize came in.

The man reached over and shook his hand. "Arnold Dolman, Chief of Police."

"Cole Shepherd, sir."

Chief Dolman placed a comforting hand on Erica's shoulder. "I'm sorry," he said softly before taking a seat at the head of the table.

It was clear the two knew each other. Then again, Cole

shouldn't be surprised since she knew Officer Durant as well.

The chief motioned toward Baker. "Bring us up to speed, please."

"Of course." Baker looked around the table. "The victim —Bethany Massy's—car was found in the woods on the edge of town. The only reason it was spotted was because another motorist stopped to change a tire, wandered into the trees a ways when nature called, and saw the vehicle." He glanced at Erica, his expression softening. "Bethany was killed with a single gunshot to the chest. An autopsy will be done, and we may get more information at that point. From the initial investigation, it looks like she was likely killed somewhere else, and then placed in the car and driven to the disposal location."

Erica sat, her spine straight and her hands clasped tightly in her lap. "Her keys were missing, weren't they?"

Durant nodded. "Yes. Her purse was still in the car, along with her phone and even her wallet. But the keys were nowhere to be found. Given the fact that someone used a set of keys to get into your place, I think we can safely assume that the killer—or killers—took them from the crime scene."

"Why her?" Erica ran her fingers through her hair. "I'm sure there were many opportunities for them to come after me instead, especially before we suspected anything was going on." She locked her fingers behind her head and tipped it back in frustration. "None of this makes any sense!"

Chief Dolman leaned forward, his arms resting on the table. "Erica, can you think of anyone who might want to hurt you? Or get back at you for any reason? Maybe a disgruntled customer."

"No. That's what's so frustrating. I've never been threatened before. The worst thing that's happened in the last three months is that I got a one-star review from a guest who was upset that there wasn't a Starbucks within a mile."

"I know this is a long shot," Durant began, "but have there been any guests that seemed secretive? Maybe someone who might have hidden something at the B&B, something the suspects are trying to find."

It wasn't a bad suggestion. Cole had his doubts, given the great lengths the suspects had gone to keep tabs on Erica.

"I don't really get to know most of my guests past the surface pleasantries." Erica looked uncertain. "I can't say anyone stands out as being especially secretive, but then I might not have realized it. I did just have someone check out yesterday morning. He's the only other guest I've had in the past week besides Cole."

Chief Dolman looked thoughtful. "Would you mind if someone looked through his room? To see if there's anything hidden somewhere that you might not have seen?"

"Not at all. If it helps us get some answers, then I'm all for it. I did clean the room yesterday. I didn't notice anything unusual, but I wasn't looking, either."

Durant patted Erica's hand. "I'll come by this evening and have a look."

Baker cleared his throat. "I hate to ask this, but is there anyone else we should be looking at? A boyfriend? Your ex-husband?"

Pink colored Erica's cheeks. "No boyfriend. I haven't spoken to my ex-husband since the divorce, and that was before Peter was born. The man was a piece of work, but I can't imagine him killing anyone. And why all of this now? It doesn't make any sense?"

"I understand. But I'd like to see where he is now and eliminate him from the suspect pool. What's his name?"

Erica folded her hands and set them on the conference table. "Jeffery Canton." There was a coolness to her voice that was barely perceptible.

Considering the guy walked away from his wife and unborn son, Cole didn't blame her in the least. Obviously, she'd chosen to go back to her maiden name after her divorce. He wondered how much Peter knew about his father.

Cole had every intention of asking Asher to investigate Jeffery Canton as well.

It was barely eleven o'clock when Erica stepped out of the police station and into the sunshine. How was that possible? It felt like they'd been in there for hours. Her eyes burned after she'd fallen apart earlier.

She slid into the passenger seat of her rental car and let her head lean against the seat. All of this made her want to take Peter out of school and leave town. To go someplace where no one could find them.

She bit her lip to keep herself from crying again.

"Hey." Cole's voice broke through her thoughts. "Which deli did you want to go to? You mentioned soup for your brother and Megan."

Thankful for something else to focus on, and for Cole who had remembered, she cleared her throat and put her seat belt on. "Hickory Street Deli."

He programmed the GPS on his phone. "Got it."

At the deli, Erica ordered two bowls of their signature chicken noodle soup to go.

"Do you prefer turkey or ham?" Cole asked her.

She gave him a questioning look.

He pulled out his wallet. "I'm getting us lunch. You still need to eat."

She replied, and he ordered two bowls of the soup along with two turkey and cheese sandwiches to go.

Erica was in a daze as they dropped the soup off at Bryce and Megan's house. She sent them a text to let them know lunch was on the front porch. She needed to let her brother know about Bethany, but she wasn't up to fielding questions right now. Not yet.

Back at the B&B, Cole carried the food inside to the kitchen table. "I can stick around if you want company, or I can leave if you'd like to be alone."

Alone with her thoughts? That sounded like a dangerous situation right now. "No, you don't need to go." She took a deep breath in and let it out again, trying to clear her head. The smell of the food made her stomach growl. "I guess I'm hungrier than I realized."

Cole got them both a bottle of water from the fridge, then handed her a sandwich and a bowl of soup along with a spoon and napkin.

She took the lid off the soup and took a bite. It was the perfect temperature. Hot, but not too hot to eat. The comforting taste was exactly what she needed. "This is great. Thank you for lunch."

"You're welcome." He ate a spoonful and nodded his approval. "There are a lot of great restaurants in Destiny. I'm impressed."

"It's a wonderful town with a strong sense of community." Erica had no doubt that someone would set up a vigil for Bethany at the college. She desperately needed to think about something else. "How's everything going with the property?"

"The realtor said we've done all we can until the inspections have been completed."

"So you're free to go back home, then."

Cole was about to take a bite of his sandwich, but he set it back down on his paper towel and looked at her from across the table. "Technically, yes." There was something in his expression that Erica couldn't quite read.

"You don't need to stick around here any longer than necessary. I know you weren't supposed to be here this long as it is."

If he'd finished all his business, he could check out after lunch and be back in San Antonio by the end of the day. The thought made her sad. But what had she expected him to do? Rent a room at the B&B indefinitely?

"Maybe not. But I'm glad I've been able to be here to help you and Peter." He picked the sandwich back up and took a hearty bite. He chewed it thoughtfully and swallowed. "I'm not in a hurry to leave. Provided I haven't overstayed my welcome, I'd like to stick around for a few more days."

She was fully aware that he was watching her as she ate another bite of soup and then dabbed at her mouth with a napkin. "Without a manager, I'll have to close the B&B most of Saturday while I'm out of town. I'm not sure how it's going to work." Truthfully, she was considering closing the B&B for the next week or two until she got a few things figured out. She'd need to hire another manager. Although the possibility of selling the place held more appeal than ever. She had a lot to think and pray about.

"What if I told you that I'd like to go with you and Peter to the football game?"

"I'd ask if you felt obligated to go and protect us."

His eyes widened at her words. He set his bottle of water down, crossed his arms, and leaned onto the table. "There is no obligation, Erica. I don't feel like I *need* to do anything. What I *want* to do is make sure you and Peter are safe tomorrow. Spending extra time with both of you is a bonus. I've found that meeting you and your son has been the highlight of my trip to Destiny."

Her breath caught at his words and the intensity of his gaze. He meant every single word, and it sent her heart racing.

Erica didn't want to go all the way to Fredericksburg tomorrow on her own. But even more than that, she didn't want Cole to leave town. Not yet. It wasn't only because he made her feel safer. It was more than that. She just hoped they'd have a chance to figure things out after all of this was over.

"I'd like it if you came with us tomorrow. I know Peter would, too."

"Then I'll stay through the weekend at least."

Chapter Thirteen

Saturday morning, Cole woke up from his spot on the couch downstairs and stretched. He'd insisted on sleeping there until the police caught the people who had killed Bethany and who were harassing Erica. He'd expected her to object. Instead, she'd looked relieved. And really, the couch wasn't uncomfortable. In his line of work, he'd slept in vehicles or on the floor before. The couch was nothing.

He folded the bedding and then checked his e-mail on his phone. Late last night, he'd called Asher and asked for a check on Jeffery Canton. Asher was known for staying up at all hours of the night, but he often slept until noon. He would find anything and everything on Erica's ex, but Cole likely wouldn't hear from him until later.

Erica seemed certain that Jeffery had nothing to do with any of this. Since the guy hadn't been in contact in over eight years, Cole was inclined to agree. It wasn't like Erica had suddenly come into money or anything like that.

Whoever these guys were, they wanted something. And considering this had been going on for nearly a week now, they weren't in a hurry. Cole couldn't quite wrap his head around it.

He was relieved Erica had agreed to him going with her and Peter to the football game. After talking last night, they decided to leave for Fredericksburg after lunch. Erica said there was a place with an indoor miniature golf course and arcade. It'd be good for Peter to relax and have some fun. Put the stress of this last week out of his mind.

Honestly, it'd be good for Erica, too.

Officer Durant said they'd have patrols going by the B&B regularly all weekend.

Cole prayed it would be the break everyone needed. While they were gone, maybe the police would find another lead. Even better, maybe someone would try to break into the B&B again and get caught.

Several hours later, they packed all of Peter's football gear along with his backpack into Cole's truck. He offered to drive them, and since there was a mileage limit on Erica's rental car, she agreed.

As Destiny faded in the rearview mirror, Erica began to visibly relax. Instead of clutching the door handle, she moved her hands to her lap and leaned an elbow against the window. She glanced at the back seat from time to time to laugh at something Peter said.

Cole checked the rearview mirror on a regular basis. There had been no sign of the SUV or car, and no indication that anyone was following them. He had every intention of remaining vigilant the entire trip to Fredericksburg and back, but he was starting to feel a bit of relief from all the stress as well.

He'd gone to arcades with the Durham family when he was a teenager. He'd played miniature golf a couple of times on school outings. But back then, Cole had such a big chip on his shoulder, he could never quite relax and enjoy himself. He was man enough to know that's why he never felt like he fit in with the Durhams. Still didn't, if he were honest.

Doing those things now with Erica and Peter was a whole new experience. Cole showed Peter how to hold the golf club, and the boy looked up at him with a big grin. Later, when Peter was able to hit the ball through the obstacle, a sense of pride filled Cole's chest.

How many times had Gregory or even Ruth tried to reach out to Cole this way when he was staying with them, and he'd rejected them? A pang of guilt knotted itself in his stomach. He pushed the thoughts away and focused on the here and now.

It was Erica's turn to hit her ball. She was surprisingly good at the game, despite denying she'd had much experience.

When her ball went through the obstacle on the first try, Peter ran up and gave her a high five. "Great job, Mom!"

"Thanks, honey." She looped an arm around her son's shoulders and drew him in for a hug. A moment later, she lifted her chin and turned her head to look at Cole. "I think it's your turn." Her warm smile drew him in.

She was including Cole in this special moment between herself and her son. He felt nothing short of honored.

He had never considered becoming a family man. It hadn't been an option before. Being here with Erica and Peter now had him thinking about the possibility. But as soon as that thought entered his mind, he threw it right back out again.

His own life was too unstable. Goodness knew he had done everything he could to not be like his own parents. But what if those genes ran deep? Erica and Peter had already been hurt by someone before. There was no way Cole was going to put them in a position where he might cause them more pain.

Instead, he would enjoy spending time with them, do everything in his power to protect them, and then, when this was all over, he would walk away before any of them got hurt.

◎

Erica accepted a hot dog and drink from Cole with a thanks. They got to the football field early so Peter could watch the game before his and cheer for the teams. Now, he was out on the field, running hard, as she and Cole watched.

She took a bite of her hot dog. What was it about food at a football game that was just so much better than any other venue?

It had been fun playing miniature golf with Peter and Cole today. She couldn't remember the last time she'd just relaxed like that. It had certainly been a while. Then she'd watched while the guys had teamed up on a video game at the arcade. When they beat something, they both raised their hands above their heads in victory before giving each other a high five.

It was cute. And a reminder of what Peter should have: a dad. She was so incredibly thankful for her own dad and brother, who had stepped up to the plate for him. But still, it wasn't quite the same.

Peter made a fabulous tackle. Erica stood with Cole, both clapping and shouting. Peter sought them out and grinned before turning his attention back to the game.

"If you don't mind me asking, what happened between you and Jeffery?"

The question from Cole threw her off balance. She didn't talk about her ex-husband much. It wasn't because she was bitter or anything like that. It was simply because he hadn't been a part of their lives in so long that she rarely thought about him. It seemed like another lifetime ago.

She glanced around, thankful there was some space between them and the other people watching the game. She angled her body toward Cole so she didn't have to speak as loudly. "Like I mentioned, I got into a lot of trouble in high school."

It'd taken years to finally forgive herself for the worry she put her parents through. They were seriously saints through it all.

Cole shook his head. "I remember you saying that, but I still find it difficult to believe."

Erica laughed. "Well, Bryce and my parents would verify it for you. I created a stressful few years for all of them. After high school, I wasn't much better. Couldn't hold down a job. I went out drinking with friends more than once and didn't remember how I got home. It wasn't good." She studied Cole's face, trying to get a sense of whether she was freaking him out or not.

He seemed to be studying her back—watching her, listening intently, his expression open.

She took a deep breath. "And then there was Jeffery. We'd known each other for a while, and he seemed to have it all together, which was attractive at the time because it was clear I did not. I was tired of my parents getting on to me about straightening my life out. So when Jeffery proposed, it seemed like the perfect solution."

"I'll bet your family was thrilled."

She snorted. "I'm lucky I have such an understanding and forgiving family, or I would have lost them. I didn't think anything of it at the time, but Jeffery was controlling. Just like you hear about on TV, he started to isolate me from my family and friends. Yet, *he'd* disappear for days at a time. He was always on edge. I never knew if he'd come home happy or upset."

Cole finished his hot dog and tossed the paper into the cupholder on the chair arm. "Did he ever hurt you?"

"No. He never physically abused me. Looking back, there was definitely some verbal abuse. He was gone so much, I could have walked away at any time."

"But you didn't."

"No. I didn't." The memories suffused her in a shame she thought she had released years ago. "I suspected he might be into drugs or something else illegal. His income was weird—sometimes there was nothing for weeks, and then suddenly we were rolling in money."

Peter's team made a touchdown, and Erica cheered with the rest of the crowd. The pure joy on her son's face while he was out on the field made all the traveling and hours at practice worth it.

She and Cole sat down again. Erica finished her hot dog, although it had gotten cold by that point. She barely noticed. He held out a hand for her trash and combined it with his own.

They were both silent for several minutes until Cole nudged her arm with his. "So what ended up happening? I mean, obviously you're not together anymore. And you can tell me to shut up and mind my own business if you want to."

"I wish I could say I came to my senses." She shrugged. "It was Jeffery who ended it. When I found out I was pregnant, he got really agitated. He insisted that it wasn't the right time, and that he didn't have the money to support a kid. When I refused to end the pregnancy, he walked away. He sent me divorce papers in the mail two weeks later, and I never saw him again."

Erica didn't want to think about what might have happened if Jeffery hadn't left before Peter was born. Things had worked out the way they were supposed to. She had no doubt about that. While she wished Peter had a father in his life, her son was happy and well-adjusted with the male role models who cared about him. She thanked God regularly for the support system they had.

"Erica?" He waited until she met his eyes. "You are one of the bravest and strongest women I've ever known. You should be proud of how you're raising that boy out there." He nodded toward the field.

"Thank you," she said, just above a whisper.

He had no idea how much his words meant to her, especially considering the childhood he'd had to endure.

Someone a few rows behind them hollered at their kid on the field, causing Erica to jump. She chuckled and shook her head. This time, when Cole nudged her arm with his, he didn't move it back again.

Erica leaned slightly into the contact. "I'm glad you came with us today."

"I am, too."

The game lasted another half hour before Peter trudged to the stands, disappointed that his team lost. The frown didn't last long, though, when the coach mentioned pizza.

Erica was tempted to say they couldn't stay, but when Peter's face brightened, and her own stomach growled, she couldn't say no.

By the time the pizza party was over, it was already dark outside. Peter was yawning, and it took some effort for Erica not to follow suit. Apparently, she didn't hide it well enough because Cole laughed.

"Come on. Let's get you guys home." He got up from the table and started stacking their plates.

Erica grabbed her purse off the back of her chair. "Peter, let's go use the bathroom before we leave. That way we won't have to stop until we get home again."

"Okay," he agreed grudgingly. He picked his backpack up off the floor and put it on.

Erica smiled over her shoulder. "We'll be right back."

"I'll pay so we'll be ready to go when you are." He matched her smile with one of his own.

She made a mental note to pay him back for the meal. He'd bought most of their meals the last two days as it was.

The restaurant had all but emptied out when the team dispersed. She led Peter across the building to the hallway at the back where a sign indicated the restrooms would be. They separated with the agreement that they would meet each other right outside.

When Erica pushed the restroom door open again, she was just in time to see someone grabbing Peter by the wrist and trying to drag him toward the emergency exit. Even though the hallway was not well lit, Peter's wide eyes and panicked expression burned themselves into her mind.

"Mom!"

"No!" She ran forward and grabbed her son's other arm just as they were going through the door. The alarm went off, but the man dragged Peter through the doorway despite Erica's attempts to stop him. "Kick, Peter. Fight!"

Peter kicked at his kidnapper's legs and tried to bite his arm, but the man didn't so much as hesitate.

The emergency door slammed shut behind them, but the alarm continued to sound.

When Erica tried to pry the man's hand off her son, he raised his other arm and backhanded her across the face. He continued to drag Peter—and her—around the corner to the back of the restaurant. When she finally got a good look at him, she was certain she'd never seen him before. He stared back at her with eyes devoid of emotion as he looped an arm around Peter's chest and gripped his shoulder.

"Why are you doing this?" She was scared to death, but somehow her voice sounded steady. Fierce. Her injured cheek ached, and blood dripped off her chin and onto the front of her shirt. "What do you want with us?"

"Your son is coming with me. Don't make me kill you in front of him. Maybe you don't care, but I'll bet your kid does."

Every warning bell—every ounce of instinct she had—told her not to let this man take Peter. She had no doubt that if she lost him now, she'd never see him again.

"Mom?" Peter's voice trembled.

"It's going to be okay."

The man's expression hardened. "No, it's not. Let go of the boy." In one motion, he shoved Peter at her and yanked a gun from the waist of his pants. He aimed it at her chest.

Erica shifted Peter around until he was behind her and steeled herself.

Chapter Fourteen

When the emergency exit alarm went off, Cole sprinted to the hallway where the restrooms were just in time to see the door leading outside slam shut. He pulled his gun from the holster at his back and then pushed the emergency door open, the continuous alarm masking the sound.

He couldn't see Erica and Peter, but a demanding voice came from the back of the building.

"Let go of the boy."

Without hesitation, weapon at the ready, Cole rounded the corner.

A man had a gun aimed at Erica's chest. She stood in front of Peter, her back straight. Anger and determination sparked in her eyes as blood dripped down her cheek. At that moment, Cole had no doubt she would die before she'd allow the man to take her son.

"Put the gun down." Cole's words echoed off the brick building behind him.

The kidnapper spared a quick glance at him, but his aim never wavered. "Take one step closer, and I'll kill her."

A black SUV rounded the building and screeched to a stop. At the same time, the door at the back of the restaurant swung open. An employee walked through the doorway with a bag of trash in his hand. He stopped short the moment he realized what was happening. The trash fell to his feet, and his arms shot into the air.

The combination was just enough of a distraction. The kidnapper's hand wavered. As soon as the gun dropped enough, Cole aimed for the man's core, held his breath and squeezed the trigger.

The kidnapper dropped his gun and crumpled to the ground.

The SUV surged forward and peeled away from the scene. Cole had a good view of the license plate number and memorized it as the vehicle disappeared around the side of the restaurant, leaving the injured man behind.

Cole ran forward and kicked the gun away from him. The man was unconscious, but Cole could tell he was still breathing. His priority right now was to get Erica and Peter somewhere safe.

He kept his gun trained on the fallen man. "Are you guys okay?" He saw Erica's bloodied face, and anger tinted his vision.

"I think so." Her voice shook, but she turned to examine Peter, and the next time she spoke, her voice was more certain. "We're okay."

"Good. Go back inside. Stay away from the windows, and call the police." He nodded toward the young employee. "You. Bring me some towels."

With wide eyes, the kid nodded and nearly beat Erica and Peter to the door.

These men had been harassing Erica for a week and had followed them all the way to Fredericksburg. They weren't going to give up now. Cole had no way of knowing if the SUV would circle back again, and he wanted Erica and her son inside where they would be safer.

Blood pooled beneath the kidnapper, and Cole bit back a curse. The guy was going to die if he didn't do something about it.

The employee returned with an armful of towels.

Cole motioned for him to drop them on the ground. "Good. Get back inside and wait for the police to arrive."

The employee ran back to the building as Cole holstered his weapon and reached for a towel. He bunched it up and pressed it against the bullet wound in the man's chest to slow the steady flow of blood. He needed this guy to stay alive. Not just because Cole hated the idea of taking someone's life, but because finding out who the kidnapper was might give them some answers.

Sirens sounded in the distance and grew louder quickly. Two police cars came into view with an ambulance behind them.

Cole immediately raised both hands as officers got out of the cars, weapons drawn. "I'm administering first aid. This man attempted to kidnap a young boy in the restaurant and threatened his mother with a gun. That's his weapon there." He nodded toward the gun on the ground. "I'm the one who shot this man to prevent the kidnapping. My gun is in a holster on my right side."

One officer retrieved the gun from the ground while another confiscated Cole's.

Emergency personnel took over care of the fallen kidnapper. "My identification and concealed carry license are in my wallet in my back, left pocket. May I get it for you?"

One of the officers nodded his permission while another

went inside the restaurant. Cole slowly withdrew his wallet and handed it over as two more officers joined them.

Over the next hour, everyone was questioned about the chain of events, and statements were given. The employee's eyewitness account combined with footage from the security cameras behind the restaurant verified their story.

Cole accepted his wallet back with a nod of thanks. "This is part of an ongoing investigation that originated in Destiny. Let me give you the name of both the chief of police as well as the officer who has been in direct contact with Erica."

The local police department seemed thankful for the information. Cole had found that, when working with local law enforcement, it was always best to be upfront.

"We'll need to keep your handgun as part of the investigation." The first officer on the scene, Lieutenant Patton, gave Cole a sympathetic look.

"I understand completely. Were they able to get any identification from the kidnapper? Do you know if it looks like he's going to make it?"

Patton shook his head. "Very little is known at this time."

Cole suspected they wouldn't have told him anyway. Hopefully, Durant or Chief Dolman will be able to get more information later.

Erica had called Durant directly with a detailed account of what happened. Then she'd spoken to Bryce to fill him in.

Patton turned to face Erica and Peter. "Are you sure you don't need further medical attention?"

The two were sitting at a table, and Erica had an arm around her son's shoulders. He was leaning against her and, as far as Cole knew, hadn't said a word once he'd told the police what happened.

An EMT had used butterfly bandages to close the gash on her cheek. Peter complained about his wrist hurting after the kidnapper yanked the boy around. The EMT wrapped an ACE bandage around it as well.

"I'm sure. Thank you." She offered the officer a tired smile.

"In that case, I don't think we need anything else at this time. I'm sorry this happened to you, ma'am. I'll be sure to get in contact with the Destiny Police Department. Hopefully we can get this resolved as soon as possible."

The rest of the police left then, and the restaurant fell silent. All the employees had been sent home a while ago when the restaurant officially closed. Now only the manager remained, but from the way she kept pacing back and forth between the kitchen and the front counter, it was clear she was ready for them to leave, too. Cole couldn't blame her.

Erica and Peter looked exhausted. He needed to get them somewhere safe for the night. The kidnappers expected them to go back to Destiny. Between here and there was a long stretch of highway that wasn't anywhere close to a town, and he couldn't risk heading that way. Cole needed to stay one step ahead.

He lifted his phone and made eye contact with the manager. "I'm going to make one last call, and then we'll get out of your hair."

She gave him a relieved nod.

Cole took a seat on the bench across the table from Erica and Peter.

He dialed a number and then hit the speaker button.

"Hey, Cole, what's up?"

"Mac, we're in a predicament and could use some assistance." Cole set the phone on the table. He relayed everything that happened at the restaurant, including having shot one of the guys from the SUV.

Mac grunted. "Predicament is a bit of an understatement. What do you need?"

"I need Asher to run the plates of the SUV." He recited the number. "See if he can link the vehicle to anyone with a record. I want to know who I shot. Erica has friends in the Destiny Police Department. They may be our best bet in getting information from the Fredericksburg department."

"Trust me, Cole. We'll do some digging. You need a spot to crash?" Mac spoke to someone in the background, but Cole couldn't quite make out the words.

"Yep. Someplace out of the way and not under my name."

"Got it. Give me a minute here."

Erica listened intently as she picked at some dried blood on her hand.

"All right." Mac gave them the name and location of a hotel that was off the highway but not too far. "I'm going to rent the hotel under my name and meet you there with a different vehicle. You need to ditch that truck. I'll make sure the room is paid up for several days, and you can lay low there while we get this figured out."

"Thanks, man. I appreciate it. And Mac? I'm going to need a handgun."

"I've got you covered. See you in about thirty minutes. Stay safe."

The call ended.

Erica met Cole's eyes and gave him a small nod. To her credit, she didn't ask why they weren't going back to Destiny. Instead, she pushed through her exhaustion and put on a smile for her son. "You ready to go to a hotel and get some sleep?"

She was going to need that strength because Cole didn't think this was even close to over.

⊚

Erica chose to sit with Peter in the back seat of the truck. He hadn't said much since the attempted kidnapping. She couldn't stop watching him and reassuring herself that he was safe. Things could have ended very differently—they nearly had.

They'd only been in the truck ten minutes when Peter leaned against her shoulder and fell asleep. Poor sweetie. Her eyes filled with tears as she brushed the hair back from his forehead. He didn't so much as shift.

Erica touched Cole's shoulder with her free arm and met his questioning look in the rearview mirror. "Peter is sleeping. Are we safe?"

"I haven't seen the SUV since the restaurant, and there's no sign of anyone else following us."

"Good." She looked out the windows. She didn't recognize any of the landmarks, but then again, it was dark outside and difficult to see much. "I've never been to Boerne before."

It was just outside San Antonio, a city she'd only been to once or twice.

"It's not far from where Durham Security operates right now. With any luck, losing a man will set these guys back. Who knows how many other people are involved? Going back to Destiny the same way we came was going to put us in the middle of nowhere with a target on our backs."

She figured as much. Going in a different direction was

smart. Still, traveling farther away from Destiny and everyone she knew made her uneasy. Her thoughts shifted to her brother. It'd been good to talk to him, but he was worried about her, and rightfully so.

Everything that happened tonight began to replay itself in her mind. She felt a little better knowing one of the men was in police custody now. But what happened earlier made her stomach roil. If she hadn't come out of the restroom when she did... She shook the horrible thoughts from her head.

"Erica?"

Cole's voice made her jump, and Peter shifted and leaned against the door. She met Cole's gaze in the rearview mirror.

"Are you all right?"

She shrugged, even though he likely couldn't see the movement in the dark. "I'll be fine." Eventually.

The worst damage wasn't physical. There were going to be a lot of sleepless nights ahead for both her and Peter.

She needed a change of subject. "Bryce wanted me to text him when we get to the hotel so he knows we made it safely." How long would it be before she saw him again? Surely only a day or two.

"It's nice you guys are so close," Cole said. "I envy that."

"I take it you and Mac aren't?"

She wasn't sure he heard her until he finally responded. "Not like that."

There was clearly more to the story, but now wasn't the time to press for details.

They rode in silence the rest of the way to Boerne, Texas, and the hotel where Mac had reserved a room. Mac texted a room number, which Erica read aloud, and Cole drove right up to it. The moment the engine was off, the hotel room door opened, and a large man stepped outside. Erica couldn't really see his face since the light in the room backlit his form, but it was clear he was built like Cole but maybe a good six inches taller.

Cole got out of the truck, and the men shook hands. He came around and opened the door on Peter's side. "Come on, buddy, let's get you inside."

Peter nodded once, released his seatbelt, and reached for his backpack. Cole helped him out, then offered Erica a hand. She gratefully took it. Her cheek throbbed with each movement.

Once they were out of the truck, Cole reached in and retrieved his backpack from the floorboard, along with a red first aid kit.

Mac was waiting in the doorway. As soon as they were inside, he closed it again.

Erica took in the room. There were two queen-sized beds, a large dresser with a TV resting on top of it, a small couch against one wall, and a tiny table in the corner with two chairs. It was nicer than a lot of hotel rooms she'd been in.

When Mac saw Erica's face and the bandage around Peter's wrist, his frown deepened. "I'm Mac Durham. I'm sorry to meet you both under these circumstances."

"I'm Erica, and this is Peter." She put an arm around her son's shoulders. "Thank you for your help."

"Of course. Our sister, Liv, threw together some spare clothes. They're in the bag on the bed. I brought some food as well." Mac turned to Cole and handed him a small gun case. "Here you go. I need to get your truck away from here ASAP." He handed Cole something else. "These are the keys to the car out front and the passkey for the hotel room. As soon as I relocate your truck, I'll be back. I rented the adjoining room. I'll let you know when I get back. Stay safe."

"I will. Thanks, Mac."

With a final nod, Mac left, and Cole closed and locked the door behind him.

"He seems nice," Erica commented. "Do you two usually work together?"

"Not often, but when there are as many unknowns as we're dealing with, it's good to have backup." Cole stood and positioned a chair in front of the adjoining rooms. "I'll move it again once I know Mac is over there."

She nodded. It made sense. But now there were two men from Durham Security working to keep her and Peter safe. "Cole? I don't know that I can afford to pay for everything you guys are doing."

He looked surprised at first, and then he frowned. "I'm not asking you to, and neither is Mac. You're not a paying client. You're a friend who needs help. I don't turn my back on friends."

She nodded, the tears in her eyes giving the dim hotel room lights a blurry halo. "Thank you." She led Peter to one of the two queen-sized beds and had him sit down. "Let me see your arm, honey."

He offered it to her with a wince. He was able to wiggle his fingers, even if it clearly wasn't pleasant. "I think it's just bruised." She looked up at Cole. "Do you agree?"

"I do." He opened the first aid kit he'd brought in and pulled out a cold pack. After activating it, he pressed it to Peter's wrist. "This will help with the swelling. I've got extra supplies in here. We can unwrap it and check it in the morning."

Peter moved his fingers a little and nodded. "Thank you."

"You're welcome." Cole put a hand on the boy's shoulder. "You were really brave back there. I'm proud of you."

Peter looked at him and then over at Erica. His eyes teared up, and his chin quivered.

Erica sat beside him on the bed and pulled him into her arms. "I know, honey. You are safe now. We will never let anyone take you." They would have to do so over her dead body.

Chapter Fifteen

As Erica comforted her son, Cole took stock of the room. She was right. He wouldn't allow anything to happen to Peter—or Erica. One way or another, they were going to figure out who was behind this and stop them. Until then, it would be a good idea to keep the duo hidden.

What he couldn't figure out was how there'd been no sign of anyone tailing them all day, and yet they were waiting in the back of the restaurant for the perfect opportunity. Had the SUV been driving around looking for them? Or was Cole so busy enjoying his time with Erica and Peter that he missed something? The last thought bothered him most of all.

Once Peter calmed down, Erica asked him if he'd like to watch some TV. He nodded and swiped at the remaining tears with the back of his hand. She set him up on the bed farthest from the door, turned on the TV, and found some cartoons. Cole wasn't overly experienced with kids, but Peter seemed exhausted. Between the football game, the trauma, and the lateness of the hour, it was no wonder.

Erica stood watching her son, her back to Cole. She was hugging herself and looking entirely too vulnerable.

He placed his hands on her shoulders. "You're an amazing mom. He's here. Safe. And we're going to keep it that way."

She nodded and sniffed.

He touched a piece of her hair, crispy with dried blood. "I know the EMT said not to shower tonight or get your bandages wet. Do you want some help getting cleaned up a bit?"

With another glance at Peter, she followed Cole to the bathroom. When she saw her own face in the mirror, she gasped. Dried blood covered the right side of her face from the cheekbone down to her jawline and dyed the ends of her hair crimson.

He ran water in the sink until it was warm, soaked a washcloth, and carefully washed the blood from her skin and hair. Pink-tinged droplets fell onto her shirt. He had been giving his report to one officer while Erica had recounted events with another. "What actually happened to your cheek?"

Erica shivered and brought her shoulders up to her ears. "I was trying to get him to loosen his grip on Peter, so he backhanded me."

Cole's jaw tightened. Someone's knuckle had collided with her smooth skin hard enough to leave a gash that really should have been closed with a couple of stitches. He gently touched her cheek near the wound. "I'm sorry I didn't go back into the hallway with you guys. If I had, I could have prevented this."

Her eyes widened as though she couldn't believe what he was saying. "It's because of you that I'm still alive and that Peter is sitting in the other room watching cartoons. If you hadn't come along when you did..." She released a slow breath as though she were trying to steady her emotions. "You saved our lives."

He took in her beautiful blue eyes before his gaze shifted to her lips. The sudden need to kiss her swept through him, and it took everything in him to keep from following his instincts. He dropped the hand that had been touching her cheek and warmed the washcloth again before cleaning the area nearest the cut.

Erica inhaled with a hiss.

"I'm sorry." He glanced at her eyes. "I'm almost done." He considered using a piece of gauze and some tape to cover the butterfly bandages, but with the location of the cut, it likely wouldn't stay anyway. "We'll need to apply more antibiotic cream every so often to keep it from getting infected. When we get back to Destiny, you should see a doctor. Stitches might do a better job of closing it up."

She turned and inspected her face in the mirror as she touched the red skin around the wound. "That looks a lot better." Her gaze shifted to him. "What about you?"

The question caught Cole off guard.

"What do you mean?"

"Are you okay? You had to shoot someone today. That can't be an easy thing to deal with."

Those captivating eyes of hers held his attention. "I had no choice."

She was right, though. It wasn't the first time he'd had to shoot a man, and in his line of work, it wouldn't be the last. He didn't regret it because it was the only way to keep everyone else safe. However, the image of the man falling to the ground was one he would never forget. He sincerely hoped he survived. "I don't enjoy having to shoot anyone.

But sometimes it can't be helped. I would do it again if it meant keeping Peter—and you—safe."

Erica turned slowly to look at him. She reached out, placing a soft hand on his arm. "Thank you," she whispered.

He wasn't sure if she took a step forward, if he did, or if it was a combination of the two. Either way, she now stood mere inches away. Her fragrance, a mixture of vanilla and something uniquely her, teased his senses.

There were a million reasons to move back. He might have even been capable of it until her gaze dropped to his mouth. He cupped her elbow with his hand and leaned in, giving her plenty of time to let him know if he was reading this wrong.

Instead, she rocked to her tiptoes. Cole didn't hesitate to meet her the rest of the way, touching her lips with his. The kiss was tentative at first, but when she stepped into his arms, he pulled her close and deepened the kiss. Everything about it felt right. As though she filled a spot that he hadn't realized was empty.

He broke the kiss, his hand still resting on her hip, and they stared at each other. He focused on catching his breath. Watching Erica do the same gave him a feeling of satisfaction that he couldn't quite describe.

Yet, considering where he was in life, kissing her had been a mistake. Cole knew it. And as soon as Erica thought things through, she would come to the same conclusion. He wasn't ready for that, though. Not yet.

He kissed her again. This time, it was filled with intensity, as though clinging to something that could never be, and Erica met his energy kiss for kiss.

"Mom?"

The sound of Peter's voice in the other room might as well have been an auditory slap. Erica jerked back suddenly and glanced at the doorway. Her hands, which had been threaded through the hair at the base of his neck, dropped to her sides. She shot Cole an apologetic look, checked her reflection in the mirror, and left the bathroom.

Erica took in a steadying breath as she rounded the corner from the bathroom to the main room of the hotel. "Hey, honey, what is it? Are you okay?"

He'd sat up some and looked more alert than he had earlier. He glanced at the bag of snacks that sat on the small table in the corner. "I'm kind of hungry."

She chuckled. There was her sweet boy. The kid who never stopped eating because it seemed like he grew just a little more every single night.

"Well, let's see what Mac found for us," Cole's deep voice came from behind Erica. He placed a hand against her back as he passed by her.

The kisses they'd shared moments ago raced through her mind, sending heat to her face and making her heart pound.

Everything about those kisses had been perfect. What was interesting about Cole was that she felt at ease around him. Like she could be herself. She had felt it immediately, too, from the moment he first walked into her B&B. She could honestly say that had never been true when it came to Peter's father. Her relationship with Jeffery had been based on timing, and she did care for him at the time. But when he walked away, and she hadn't been devastated, she'd realized how little love was in their marriage.

Not that she was in love with Cole. That seemed impossible. She'd only known him a week, and he was leaving

Destiny as soon as he no longer had to keep saving her and Peter. If it hadn't been for this mess, he probably would have left a day or two ago.

Guarding her heart was not only a good idea, but it was also a necessity. Still, even knowing whatever attraction this was between them couldn't go anywhere, she couldn't find it in her to regret kissing him.

Cole picked up the bag of snacks and dumped it out on the bed in front of Peter. It was an impressive variety. There were granola bars, bags of chips, packages of jerky, pouches of applesauce, and even candy bars.

Erica knew her son well and quickly made her suggestion. "It's getting pretty late, honey. Why don't you have a granola bar and some applesauce? You can have some of the other snacks tomorrow."

Peter's gaze lingered on a bag of chips, but he nodded and grabbed the snacks she'd mentioned.

Erica picked up the bag of clothing that Mac said Livi had put together. "Did you say Livi is the youngest of the Durham family?"

"Well, tied for youngest. She and Asher are twins." Cole walked over and stood beside her.

"The computer guru." She picked up a boy's T-shirt and set it aside for Peter to change into in the morning.

Cole chuckled, and the sound of his voice washed over her.

"Yes, he's our resident computer expert." He held out a granola bar. "Do you want something to eat?"

"No, thank you. I'm not even remotely hungry." She glanced at him to find he was watching her carefully. She turned back to the clothes and found a blouse that would fit her. "I'm going to go change into this since mine looks like something you'd find at a Halloween party."

"The blood stands out, doesn't it? Go ahead. I'll keep an eye on Peter."

Once in the bathroom again, she locked the door behind her and changed shirts. Between the dried blood and a tear at the hem, Erica promptly threw her old shirt into the trash can.

She looked in the mirror and decided that it was definitely an improvement. Only then did she notice the wrapped toothbrushes, toothpaste, deodorant, and even a hairbrush resting on the countertop.

Wow, Mac and Livi really had thought of everything.

Erica reached for the brush and ran it through her hair. She hadn't realized how tangled it was until she had to work through the snags.

She set the brush back down and braced both hands on the countertop, then began to pray in a hushed voice. "Thank you, Father, for getting us here safely. Thank you for being with us, for providing for us, and for sending Cole to protect us." She drew in a slow breath and let it out again. "Give us wisdom to know what to do. Help us to find a way out." Her thoughts shifted to Cole. "Protect my heart, Father."

Feeling a little more human, she exited the bathroom to find Cole lounging on the bed with Peter, both laughing at the antics on TV.

Cole pointed to the screen. "You really can't beat Scooby Doo. They just don't make cartoons like they used to." He glanced at Erica. "Feel better?"

"Yeah, I do." She went around the bed and sat on the edge next to Peter. "And you're right. Cartoons these days are just weird."

"I got a text from Mac," Cole began. "He's back and getting settled next door."

Erica noted that the chair had been moved, allowing access to the door between the rooms. She turned her attention back to the guys.

Peter had finished his granola bar and was nearly done with the applesauce. He was watching cartoons and laughing, but his eyes betrayed how tired he was.

"After this episode is over, you need to brush your teeth and get some sleep."

Peter didn't argue with her or even act disappointed, confirming her suspicion.

Thirty minutes later, she moved his backpack to a nearby chair and tucked him into bed. Even though he was exhausted, he seemed a little apprehensive, so she laid down with him. It didn't take long for him to close his eyes and drift off to sleep.

Erica reached over and brushed some hair off his forehead. Just having him lying there next to her, the gentle sounds of his breathing filling the space between them, was a miracle after today. One she didn't want to ever take for granted.

When he was sound asleep, she carefully scooted off the bed and stood. Muscles in her arms and back protested, sore after the literal tug-of-war from earlier.

"You should try to get some rest, too," Cole said. He was reclining on the other bed, an e-reader in his hands.

"What about you?" Surely he wasn't going to stay awake all night. Although she knew she would sleep better if he did.

"Mac and I will take turns staying on duty. Trust me, I'm used to operating on little sleep for days. I've got this." He gave her a reassuring smile. There was something else in his expression that she couldn't quite decipher—an unspoken question that he seemed afraid to voice.

Erica more than understood because she was in the same boat. What did the kisses mean? Was he still planning on leaving the private security firm? Would he ever consider staying in Destiny? The questions were too weighty to even think about tonight.

A quiet knock on the door between their room and Mac's snagged both of their attention. Cole stood up and went over to open it.

Mac stepped into the room, noticed Peter sleeping, and said in a quiet voice, "I've got some updates for you guys."

Chapter Sixteen

Erica requested that they talk in the same room where Peter was sleeping, so Cole moved the small table to the other side of the room, and Mac brought in an extra chair. He couldn't blame Erica for wanting to keep an eye on her son after everything they'd been through.

Cole retrieved a bottle of water for each of them, then got into the caramel Twix stash in his backpack and handed one to Erica.

"Thank you. This is one of my favorite candy bars."

Mac raised an eyebrow at their common affinity for the same candy bar but waved the candy away. He'd never been a big fan of caramel.

"You sure we're not going to wake him up?" Mac tilted his head toward Peter's sleeping form on the other side of the room.

Erica shook her head. "Once he's out like this, it takes a lot to wake him up. What updates do you have?"

That seemed to satisfy Mac. "We're still trying to get

the identity of the man Cole shot. They transported him to the hospital."

"Good." Cole was relieved the man survived. He really didn't want to have killed someone, but also because he hoped they might get some information out of the guy.

Erica lifted a Twix bar. "We know people at the police department in Destiny who are working on his identity. I'm supposed to check in with them in the morning to see if there's any information."

Cole would make a mental note to have Erica call once they were all up and going in the morning. Unfortunately, since the incident happened late this evening, it would probably take some time tomorrow for the Destiny Police Department to get any answers. "Since the case began in Destiny, I'd like to think the Fredericksburg police will be cooperative."

"I sure hope so. That SUV didn't just disappear." He scratched the back of his neck. "After they went to so much effort to follow you to Fredericksburg and try to kidnap Peter, I'm surprised they didn't come after you when you left the restaurant. too."

"So am I." Most likely, losing one of their own meant they needed to regroup. "This whole situation doesn't feel right. It's not your typical kidnapping attempt."

"We haven't been able to come up with a clear connection on our end, either," Mac turned to Erica. "We did do some research on your ex-husband, Jeffery Canton. It seems he's been living in the Houston area since about six months after your divorce. He's had a variety of jobs ranging from working at a tire repair shop to a taco stand. It doesn't look like he's maintained any of them for longer than a few months to a year."

Erica set down her half-eaten Twix. "I still can't see him

being a factor in this. Why would he send guys to kidnap Peter? It makes no sense at all. I mean, he's his biological father. Why not just try to get custody instead?"

"Maybe he feels like that would never happen since he's been absent for so long?" Cole suggested.

Mac held up a finger. "Given his history, there's no way he could gain custody of Peter. Jeffery Canton has an extensive criminal record, including drug possession and robbery. He's been in jail three different times. This last stint ended not two weeks ago."

Erica stared at the small table between them. She picked up a crumb and rolled it between her thumb and forefinger, a frown deepening the crease between her brows. "I'd suspected drugs might be in play while we were married, but..." She shrugged. "It still makes me sad to hear that."

She continued to twiddle with the crumb, and Cole resisted the urge to reach for her hand. "What was he in jail for this last time?"

"Drug possession with intent to sell." Mac looked at some notes on his phone. "He got out after six months on a technicality."

"It's a bit of a coincidence that he's released from jail, and a week later, people start harassing you. The motive isn't clear, but the timing is pretty suspicious." Cole took a long drink of his water. "At the same time, he doesn't seem to be in a position financially to hire a group of goons."

"Unless he's deeper into the drug scene than we realized," Mac suggested.

"You mean he might be caught up in drug trafficking?" Erica's voice was quiet. It was clear she wasn't sold on the idea. "I can't see it."

"Where is he now?" Cole was half tempted to drive to Houston and question the guy himself.

"That's just it. I don't know." Mac frowned. "As far as we can tell, he hasn't been back to his last known residence since he was released from jail. He hasn't checked in with his parole officer, either. It's like he was released from jail and disappeared into thin air."

Erica finished her candy and leaned back in her chair. "None of this makes any sense." She rubbed her forehead with her fingers. "We know they tried to take Peter. Not me. Not both of us. Peter. Why? And was that the plan all along, even when they were snooping around the B&B?" She shivered and crossed her arms in front of her.

Cole had noticed a light jacket tucked into the bag of clothing Liv sent. He retrieved it and held it out for Erica so she could slip her arms into the sleeves.

She gave him a nod of thanks.

"The fact that they specifically tried to take Peter is why I'm really curious about Jeffery Canton," Mac admitted. "Since they've been harassing you two for a while, it wasn't a random attempted kidnapping. There's a reason they chose you and Peter."

"And that's what we need to figure out. Because it doesn't look like they're going to quit. And we know now that they're willing to kill to get him." Cole sat down and mentally went through everything that happened at the restaurant. "It was bold to go after Peter in the open like that. It reeks of desperation." And desperate men were often difficult to predict, meaning it made his job to protect Erica and her son even harder.

The three sat in silence for several moments, punctuated by Erica's yawn.

They weren't going to be able to figure anything else out tonight.

Cole brushed his fingers across the back of her hand. "You should get some sleep."

She looked like she wanted to argue, but a second yawn must have convinced her. She pushed away from the table. "I can't thank either of you enough for what you're doing." Her chin quivered slightly. "I hope you guys can get some rest, too."

She carefully climbed under the covers in the bed next to Peter, shifting to curl her arm beneath her pillow, her back to the men. Cole switched off all the lights except the one in the bathroom.

Mac motioned for him to join him near the doorway between their rooms so they could talk between them without disturbing the Keyes family.

"Hey, is there anything you want to talk to me about?" Mac leaned against the doorframe.

Cole raised an eyebrow. "I get the sense you're referring to something specific."

The first thing that popped into his mind was his growing interest in Erica. But there were a lot of things his half-brother could be referring to.

"How about why you so readily volunteered to go to Destiny and look for property in the first place? Come on, Cole. You're the first one to jump on a new case. I've never seen anyone who kept themselves as busy as you do. Volunteering to do something boring and mundane is a huge red flag."

Ruth often worried about the same thing. In her motherly way, she'd remind Cole that it was important to rest sometimes. But staying busy—mentally and physically—had been how Cole managed his childhood, and that coping mechanism stayed with him as he grew up. He didn't know how else to approach life, so he could see why volunteering to step away from working cases to look for property in Destiny might make others wonder.

He'd hoped to avoid the topic until after he'd made his final decision. Mac knew him too well, though. There was no delaying the conversation now.

Cole leaned against the wall behind him. "I'm considering leaving Durham Security once you guys relocate. I guess I figured checking out the properties would give me some distance. Perspective." He shrugged.

"You're thinking about stepping away from private security in general? Or just from our company?" There was no accusation, only a search for the truth.

"Originally, I thought about stepping away entirely. But then Erica and Peter needed my help, and I realized that what I do—what we do—isn't something I can just leave behind."

Cole knew Mac understood. They'd spoken about this very topic before. For better or worse, the drive to protect those who were being threatened was something they all had in common.

Mac didn't say a word, but his expression spoke volumes. Cole shifted his weight from one foot to the other. Very few people had the ability to shake him up, but Mac was one of them. He wasn't sure if it was his commanding presence, that Mac was older by two years, or if it was the fact that he was really Cole's only blood relative, even if only half. Most likely, it was a combination.

When Cole returned silence with silence, Mac gave him a stern look. "I've lost count of how many times I've told you that you're one of us, man. There's nothing I can say or do to convince you of that. Your strange determination to believe otherwise is a 'you' problem."

How many times had they had a similar discussion? Sure, Mac had a stepmom, and his other siblings were all half-siblings, but at least they'd known him since they were born. Plus, Mac had his dad there.

Cole was the one who entered the family as a teenager. He disrupted everything with his bad attitude and the giant chip on his shoulder. He put the family through a lot. There was no way they didn't still see that when they looked at him. He never felt like a Durham.

Greg had little choice in taking Cole in. After all, the Durham family couldn't turn their backs on someone in need.

He'd considered himself an obligation, and he'd joined the family business to pay them back for all they'd done for him growing up. The change in business location was a natural time to break away.

Mac must have realized that was the end of the conversation, so he switched directions. "Erica is an impressive woman, isn't she?"

"She sure is. Been through a lot and still keeps her chin up." He admired that about her. Truth was, Cole kept finding more and more things to like about Erica.

"You care about her and the boy." It wasn't a question.

And there was no use denying it. "Yep. It wasn't the plan, and I'm not real sure what to do about it."

"If you move to Destiny, whether you stick with the business or not, it would kind of open up your options." Mac shrugged innocently. "I'm just saying."

Cole chuckled at that. "You're like a bulldog with a bone."

"Comes in handy sometimes." Mac grinned back. "You know what Mom would say, right?"

Cole groaned as the quote immediately came to mind.

"If you put more thought than heart into falling in love, then you're not doing it right," they said in unison.

Ruth was known for saying it every time one of her kids even thought about entering into a new relationship. Now that all the kids were older, she and Gregory seemed to worry that none of them were going to get married and give them the grandbabies they wanted so badly.

The men laughed together.

Mac pushed away from the doorframe. "Go get some sleep. I'll take the first watch. You've been through the wringer today, too."

"I appreciate it. I'm leaving the door open. Just come wake me up when you're ready to switch."

"Will do." Mac clapped him on the shoulder and went into his room.

Cole kicked his shoes off, plugged his phone in on the table between the two beds, and lay down. He listened to the peaceful sound of Erica and Peter's deep breathing and prayed they could find whoever was after them before anyone else got hurt.

Chapter Seventeen

When Mac woke Cole for his shift a few hours later, Cole dragged himself out of bed and immediately put his shoes on. Mac headed for his room where he would likely drop into a sound sleep.

Cole wished he had a giant cup of coffee. Instead, he got another Twix out of his backpack and claimed a spot on the couch. Before he even had a chance to open the candy bar, he could hear Mac snoring from the other room.

Erica shifted restlessly and finally rolled over to face his direction. Cole was surprised when she got up and quietly tiptoed across the room to the couch.

"Hey," she whispered. "Do you mind if I join you for a few minutes?"

"Of course not." He motioned to the portion of the couch that remained empty. "Having trouble sleeping?"

"Every time I go to sleep, I start dreaming..." Her gaze darted to the hotel door. "The practical side of me knows that we're fine now. But when I close my eyes, I picture the guy staring at me from the SUV before they ran us off the road. Or the same guy trying to take Peter." She shivered and rubbed her arms with her hands. "I can't take another nightmare."

Cole wanted to reassure her that they would go away once they had the men responsible behind bars. But he knew very well that wasn't something he could promise. The lasting trauma from going through an ordeal like this could continue indefinitely. Especially for Peter, but for Erica too. He could only imagine what it must have been like to literally fight for her son's life and nearly lose her own.

He shifted closer to her and extended an arm across the back of the couch. "Come here." His voice sounded slightly husky even to his own ears.

She didn't hesitate to lean in, and he wrapped his arm around her shoulders and pulled her close. With a palm against his chest, she tucked her head into his shoulder. It amazed him how perfectly she fit into that space.

Cole would have been content to simply hold her for as long as she wanted to stay. But when she lifted her chin to look at him, there was no way he could resist a second chance to kiss her. Without hesitation, he gently explored her lips with his own. The kiss only lasted a breath or two, but somehow, it felt much more meaningful than the first kisses they had shared.

He gently touched her face near the cut on her cheek. "How is it feeling?"

She gave an adorable little shrug. "It's okay. Sore, but it'll heal." She wrinkled her nose. "I hope it doesn't scar too badly. I don't think facial scars look quite as attractive on women as they do on rugged men."

"Oh, I don't know. Yours will tell the story of bravery, strength, and a refusal to quit. I find all three of those attributes to be incredibly attractive." He used a finger to sweep hair away from the cut and brushed her cheek with his thumb.

With a contented sigh, Erica rested her head against his chest. He pressed a kiss to her hair and sent up a silent prayer for guidance. Not just with regard to his job, but about Erica as well.

Minutes later, her breathing started to even out. The realization that she felt comfortable enough to fall asleep in his arms was humbling. But she needed some quality rest, and he needed to be prepared in case they got unwanted visitors.

"Hey, sleepy head. You'd better go lie down before I'm forced to carry you back to your bed," he whispered with a chuckle.

Erica nodded slowly and pushed against his chest to sit up. "It doesn't look like my brain is going to give me much choice." She covered a yawn. "Good night, Cole."

"Good night." He resisted the urge to pull her in for one more kiss. Instead, he watched in the dim light as she got into bed beside her son. For the first time, he wondered what it would be like to wake up next to someone every morning.

Cole stifled a groan.

When he decided to travel to Destiny to look for property for the Durham family, his decision whether he would stay with the company or not seemed to loom in front of him like a cliff wall. But instead of finding clarity, everything in his life had gotten infinitely more complicated.

The next morning, Erica exited the bathroom and glanced at the bed to see that Peter was still asleep. Of course, Cole was already awake since he'd been keeping watch, and Mac was sitting on the couch tying his shoes.

Mac jabbed at the door with his thumb. "They have a continental breakfast. I vote we hang onto the snacks in case we need them later. As amazing as caramel Twix are, I don't think they count as a complete breakfast." He gave Cole a teasing look. "I'll run over and bring a selection back. We'll eat breakfast, and then let's get started on those conference calls. See if we can get some answers."

With that, he left the room, and Cole locked the door behind him. "I can't imagine what they have to eat compares to what you offer at your B&B," he said. "I'd give my left pinkie toe for one of those bear claws."

Erica laughed. "I'm starving too. I hope he brings plenty back, or we'll have to make a second trip when Peter wakes up." She looked across the room at her son. From the time he could talk, he would wake up asking for food. His morning priorities hadn't changed much through the years.

Part of her couldn't wait to get home. But when she thought about the B&B, the idea of going back to the large building and being there alone with Peter made her anxious.

She startled when Cole touched her arm and swung her focus to him.

Concern knitted his brow. "You okay?"

"Yeah." Erica drew in a deep breath and released it slowly. "The more I think about it, the more certain I am about selling the B&B. I'm ready for a change. And after all this, I'm going to adopt a giant guard dog. Like Great Dane big."

She considered what it would be like to own a little three-bedroom house. There would be so much less to clean and take care of. It'd be cozy. Homey.

An image of Cole and Peter playing football in the backyard together popped into her head, and it seemed so normal that it took several heartbeats to push it aside.

She glanced at Cole and then away, hoping her cheeks didn't look as pink as they felt. "I can't even begin to fathom what it would take to move out of there. The ideal solution would be to relocate our personal things and find someone who wants to buy everything else as a package deal."

"When you're ready, maybe Tanya, the realtor, will be able to help," he suggested. "She's been easy to work with so far."

All of it sounded great, but Erica had no idea what she was going to do for employment. Maybe, if someone bought the B&B and kept it running, she could work as a manager during the day. Otherwise, she was going to have to dust off her resume. It was a scary thought.

She was thankful when a tap at the door let them know Mac had returned. Cole checked to be sure it was him first, then opened the door wide.

"I come bearing juice and packages of mini donuts," he announced. "Only a smidge healthier than a Twix bar."

Erica took the four bottles of juice—two apple and two orange—from him and set them down on the table. Mac added the pile of chocolate and powdered mini donuts.

"Does Peter have a preference?" Cole asked.

"He would definitely choose chocolate donuts and apple juice."

With a nod, Cole got one of each and put them in the mini-fridge. His thoughtfulness made Erica's heart turn over. She sat at the square table and reached for an orange juice and a package of powdered donuts. "Thank you for getting this, Mac."

"You're welcome," he said, the words slightly muffled by

the donut he was chewing. He swallowed. "Sorry, didn't mean to be rude."

She waved away the apology. "You're good."

Cole chose chocolate donuts and orange juice and then handed his burner phone to Erica. "Why don't you call Bryce first and check in, then call Officer Durant. Maybe she'll have some updates for us."

Erica's conversation with Bryce was short. He was relieved to hear they were still okay but was concerned about all that had happened since she left Destiny.

Apparently, he'd tried to sugarcoat the situation for their parents, but they had seen through it and were headed back home today. Erica was sorry they were cutting their trip short but understood. If it were Peter, she would do the same thing.

She was happy to hear that both Megan and Bryce were feeling much better, and she promised him that she'd call once they had more information.

After she hung up with Bryce, she called the Destiny Police Department and asked for Jenny, then put the phone on speaker so Cole and Mac could hear the conversation, too.

"This is Officer Durant."

"Hey, Jenny, it's Erica. I've got you on speaker with Cole and Mac Durham."

"Erica, I'm glad you called. You guys are making some serious ripples over there," she said with a hint of humor in her voice. "Why don't you update me on your situation first, and then I'll tell you what we know here."

Together, Erica, Cole, and Mac reported everything that had happened the day before.

Partway through, Peter woke up, and Erica excused

herself to get him his breakfast and encouraged him to read his book while he ate.

Jenny cleared her throat. "Okay, let me start at the beginning. First, Erica, your B&B is fine. We've had patrols going by regularly, and there haven't been any other issues. We found an abandoned SUV that was torched out near the lake. There was evidence of front-end damage consistent with how you were hit when you were run off the road. Three sets of footprints were in the mud around the SUV. There was nothing unique or significant about them, except the sizes indicated they were all men."

That meant there was probably one more person in the back of the SUV when they ran Erica off the side of the road. Knowing what she knew now, she had no doubt they'd intended to stop and kidnap Peter. Praise God that Cole had been driving right behind them. She swallowed past a lump in her throat and blinked back the tears that were gathering.

"That means the SUV used in Fredericksburg was a different one," Mac stated.

"Yes, it was." The sound of papers shuffling came over the phone as Jenny took a moment. "Here we go. I spoke with the Fredericksburg Police Department. They were very cooperative. They did get a video of the entire kidnapping attempt from the restaurant. However, the video quality is poor, and they couldn't see the driver. We ran the plate number. I don't think any of us are surprised to hear that the plates were stolen. A BOLO has been sent out to all three towns."

"How's the suspect that I shot? Last I heard, he was being taken to the hospital."

"He's out of surgery but still unconscious. The hospital staff is supposed to let the local authorities know as soon as he's awake so that he can be questioned. They were able to identify him as Juan Ramirez, twenty-eight years old. He was in and out of jail due to DUI and drug-related charges. The interesting thing is, he's not from around here. His place of residence is in Houston."

That had their attention.

"Houston." Cole looked at Erica. "Is there any record of a connection between Juan and Jeffery Canton?"

Erica still couldn't fathom her ex orchestrating any of this. At the same time, it made little sense for people to come all the way from Houston to target her and try to kidnap Peter. Right now, Jeffery was the only commonality.

"We wondered the same here," Jenny said. "There's no direct connection between the two. However, Juan reportedly worked with a man that goes by the name of Ghost. Get this—the last charge that Jeffery Canton served time for? When he was being questioned, Ghost came up in the interview. Apparently, the police in Houston are trying to track Ghost down and mention the name to anyone arrested on a drug charge. Jeffery denied knowing anything about Ghost, but the officer who conducted the interview stated that there were multiple behaviors that indicated he was lying."

"That's a pretty thin correlation," Erica said, although she couldn't deny it was there.

"You're not wrong." Jenny paused. "We've got mugshots of several of the guys who are known associates of Juan Ramirez. I'm going to text them to you. Let me know if any of you recognize them. Erica, I'm sending them to you now. You might show them to Peter, if you think he's up to it. I'd be interested to hear if one of these guys is the man who bothered him and his friends at school."

"Of course." Erica turned and called out to Peter.

"Honey, I need you to come here for a second, please."
When he hopped off the bed and joined them, Erica stood
so that he could sit down in her place. "Officer Jenny wants
us to look at some photos. If you recognize anyone, I need
you to let us know. Okay?"

"Okay." Peter sat up straighter, seeming to take his new
job seriously.

Erica's phone pinged, and she brought up the text
messages. "All right, let's go through these together." She
didn't recognize the first picture, and no one else reacted
either.

The moment Cole scrolled to the second photo, Peter
leaned forward and pointed. "That's the guy who was
talking to me, Shawn, and Axel at school. He was going to
get in trouble, but he left before the principal found out."

"Did you hear that, Officer Durant? Peter is referring to
the photo of Wallace Cash," Mac told her.

"Noted."

"All right, two more to go." Erica swiped to the next
photo. When no one responded, she swiped again to the
last one.

She recognized the man immediately. Goosebumps
peppered her skin as she stared into the face she knew
would be haunting her nightmares for a long time.

Chapter Eighteen

Cole stood. He walked around and placed a hand on Peter's shoulder and another against Erica's back. He gave Peter a gentle squeeze.

Erica set her phone down on the table. "Yes, he's the man who was sitting in the passenger seat when the SUV ran us off the road."

Cole noticed the way she leaned into his touch. He rubbed her back softly with his thumb. "If you need further confirmation, I also saw him at the football field." He bent down so he was eye-to-eye with Peter. "You did a good job, buddy."

"Yes, you did." Erica kissed his temple. "You can go back to reading your book now."

Without another word, Peter walked away and flopped on the bed again.

Erica braced her hands on the back of the chair.

"That's what I expected based on your description of the man," Jenny said over the phone. "His name is Marshal Smith. Now, there's at least one direct connection between him and Jeffery Canton. It looks like they were involved in a physical altercation at a bar almost two years ago. The police were called, and a formal report was made. In the end, neither of them pressed charges, and they both walked away."

Erica leaned forward, her hair draping in front of her face like a waterfall. She stood again with a groan. "Even with all of these connections, I don't understand what any of this has to do with Peter and me." She glanced at her son as though she were worried that their conversation might bother him.

Cole wondered if Peter even knew his father's name. Did he realize that was who they were talking about?

"I'm going to keep digging," Jenny promised. "I plan to call over to the Houston PD and speak with them about Jeffery as well as this Ghost that keeps popping up in reports. As soon as I hear back from the FPD about questioning Juan Ramirez, I'll give you a call and let you know what they say. In the meantime, we've sent his image, as well as those of the men you didn't recognize, to all participating precincts. With any luck, he'll make a wrong move, and we'll be able to bring him in. And Erica?"

"I'm here."

"You guys be careful, okay?"

"Will do. Thanks again, Jenny."

Mac reached over and ended the call. Moments later, his own phone rang. "Hey, Asher. I'm putting you on speaker." He set the phone on the table. "Okay, you're good."

"Hey, Asher," Cole greeted as he took a chair around the table.

"Cole. Man, it's good to hear your voice. You've had us all worried."

"We're holed up and okay for now," Cole assured him.

"Good to hear it. I wanted to check in and see if there

was anything I could do to help. I can head that way if you need an extra set of eyes and hands."

"There's nothing you can do here at the moment," Cole said. "We're pretty much just sitting around waiting for more information." He told Asher about what Officer Durant said and gave him the names of their known suspects plus the two associates none of them recognized.

"I'll do my own research as well," Asher assured them. "In the meantime, you guys take care of yourselves. And Miss Erica, if you're there, I hope to have the chance to meet you in person someday."

Erica seemed surprised that he mentioned her by name. "I'd like that, too. I appreciate all your help."

"Not a problem. All right, talk to you guys later."

With that, the call ended, and the room suddenly seemed way too quiet.

Mac picked up his phone and lightly tapped it against the tabletop. "So for now, we sit tight. Give everyone time to gather as much information as possible and get back to us."

"I hate waiting." Erica sat on the edge of the closest bed and chewed her bottom lip.

Mac got up and sat beside her. "We do a lot of it in our line of work." He motioned to both himself and Cole and lowered his voice. "Knowing about Peter, I brought my old handheld gaming system with me. Is it okay if he plays it? I wanted to ask you first before I offered it to him."

The corners of her mouth lifted. "It'll take his mind off everything and keep him from getting bored. That was very considerate. Thank you, Mac."

She got up and went to stand beside Cole as Mac showed Peter how to use the gaming system.

"I know I haven't met the whole family, and I haven't spent a lot of time with those that I have," she kept her voice barely above a whisper, "but they seem pretty great. As far as I can see, they treat you like a brother."

"This is Durham Security, Erica. We back each other up and do what we need to do to keep our clients safe."

She shook her head as though she couldn't believe him. "I'm not a client. They're helping me and Peter, and I will forever be grateful. But they're here for *you*, Cole, because you asked them. Because they clearly see *you* as family."

With that, she kissed him lightly on the cheek and joined Mac and Peter.

He wanted to argue Erica's point. After all, how could she possibly know anything about the Durhams or his relationship with them after only a day?

And then he realized that, when he first met Bryce and Megan, he could tell they were all a close-knit family. That they would do anything and everything for each other. He'd admired that. Honestly, he'd been a bit envious.

Like that sensation when your ears clear and you can hear again, but you hadn't realized they were clogged in the first place, Cole's memory seemed to sharpen.

Recollections flooded in, all bathed in a new light.

Mac standing up for him at school not long after Cole went to live with the Durhams. Gregory introducing Cole along with his kids, and never once did he differentiate between Cole and his children by blood. When Cole got sick, Ruth brought in soup and kept checking on him, even when it drove him crazy, and he got grumpy. He could think of a similar situation with each of the younger Durham siblings as well.

What if Mac was right? What if the Durham family had never seen him as a burden or an outsider, and it was completely a problem of his own making?

"Do you want to try it now?" Peter asked as he handed the gaming console over to Cole.

"Sure. Believe it or not, I used to play this game when I was your age. Let's see how much I can remember." He was convinced playing video games was a lot like riding a bike. Thankfully, the hours he spent working his way through the levels in this one paid off.

"Wow," Peter breathed. "I hope I can get as good at this game as you are. Maybe Mom will get it for me for Christmas."

They were hanging out in Mac's room so Erica would have a chance to take a nap in the other room. She'd been nodding off for a while when he finally suggested that she lie down and get some real rest. He prayed she could sleep peacefully without nightmares. Mac was reading on the couch in the room with her, leaving Cole and Peter on their own.

"Is Mom going to be okay?"

Apparently, Cole wasn't the only one thinking about Erica.

"She's just tired, buddy. She hasn't been sleeping much lately."

Peter was the one who was nearly kidnapped, and yet he was concerned about his mom. His innocence and kind heart impressed Cole.

"You're a good son. Did you know that?"

Peter nodded slowly. "I try to take care of her, but some-times she gets sad. After Uncle Bryce and Aunt Megan got married, it seemed like they were always happy. I think my mom needs to get married too. Maybe she wouldn't be sad anymore."

Then, as if they hadn't just been talking about something an eight-year-old shouldn't be worrying about, he picked up the gaming console again and said, "I'm gonna try and beat your score."

"You do that." Cole ruffled his hair. "Do you need a snack?"

The boy nodded but never took his eyes off the screen.

Cole got to his feet and walked to the other room, relieved to see that Erica was still asleep. He glanced to his right to find Mac watching him, one eyebrow raised.

"You've got some heavy conversations going on in there," he said in a hushed tone.

"No joke." He grabbed a bottle of water and chose a bag of chips from the snacks that Mac had brought. He passed back by the couch, but Mac held up a leg and stopped him.

"The kid trusts you, and you clearly care about his mom. Maybe you should throw your hat in for the job. You're not getting any younger, you know." There was humor in Mac's eyes but a degree of seriousness as well.

It took some control not to laugh out loud. "Considering you're two years older than me, you might throw some of your crazy advice at the mirror."

"Tried it once, and it didn't stick. I don't intend to make the same mistake twice." He scowled. "Are you telling me you don't think about it sometimes? A wife. Kids. Leaving a legacy."

A quick glance at Peter assured Cole that the boy was content and entertained. "Maybe. But what we do every day isn't easy." He made sure to keep his voice at a whisper.

"True, but Dad made it work, and Mom is supportive. That means it's attainable."

Cole wanted to tease Mac about giving himself another chance to find the right woman to grow old with. But when

Cassie asked for a divorce two years into their marriage, it really hurt Mac.

Regardless, contemplating it and finding the right woman to spend your life with were two entirely different things.

As crazy as it was, he could visualize the possibility with Erica, which was scary in itself. How was it possible to care so deeply about someone in such a short time?

Erica hadn't intended to sleep for two hours, and she certainly hadn't expected to rest peacefully. If she had any dreams, she didn't remember them. Still feeling groggy, she sat up slowly and stretched.

Mac looked up from his spot at the table. "Feel better?"

"Yes, I do. Thank you. What have you been up to?"

He'd been bent over the tablet he was using earlier. He rotated it to show her a sketch that left her speechless.

Peter was sitting on the hotel bed, video game console in his hand, and he was looking up with a smile on his face.

Erica reached for the device to study the picture close up. "This is amazing, Mac. You have a real gift here."

He shrugged. "It's just a hobby. A way to pass the time."

"Well, if you didn't already have a calling, this could be it." She handed the tablet back to him. "Did I miss anything?"

"Not much. Asher's having lunch delivered any minute now. Chicken sandwiches and French fries, if I remember right." He folded the cover over on the device and set it on the table.

"That sounds great. Please thank him for me. I wish I had the opportunity to meet the rest of your family."

"Well, it looks like we'll be moving to Destiny before too long, so maybe you'll get the chance."

"I'd like that." She smiled, then turned her attention to the adjoining room where Peter and Cole were propped up against the wall on the bed watching TV. As soon as Peter saw her, he hopped off the bed and ran over. "Mom! Do you feel better now?"

Erica chuckled. "I was fine before, honey. Just tired."

He bounced up and down several times, then held out his wrapped wrist. "Can we take this off, please? It's seriously messing with my game scores."

She bit her bottom lip to keep from laughing again. "We can try it, but if it hurts very much, we need to wrap it again. Deal?"

"Deal!"

Cole strolled over. "You want some help?"

Peter thrust his arm out. "Yes, please."

Cole unwrapped Peter's little arm to reveal five angry finger-shaped bruises on his wrist. It took everything in Erica not to reach down and pull her baby into her arms.

"Can you wiggle your fingers?" Cole made the motion, and Peter copied it. "Can you make a tickle monster?" He demonstrated by creating a claw with his hand and tickling Peter's side.

Peter erupted in giggles and shook his head.

"All right, it looks like your arm is okay. But like your mom said, if it starts bothering you again, you need to tell her."

"I will." With that, he bounded across the room, flopped onto the bed, and scooped up the game console.

A tap at the door announced the arrival of their lunch.

By the time it was afternoon, Erica had had enough sitting around, so she got busy cleaning the hotel room up a little. It was amazing how much damage four people could do in less than a day.

She had just wiped off the table when her cell phone finally rang. She answered it immediately.

"Hello?" The familiar voice of Jenny made her hopeful. "Absolutely. Let me put you on speaker."

The three adults sat around the table again so they could all hear. "Hey, everyone. I hope you're all hanging in there this afternoon. Look, I won't keep you waiting. I've got two interesting pieces of information to pass along."

Mac pulled out an electronic notebook and was getting ready to write on it.

"I had a long conversation with several people at the Houston Police Department. The last time Jeffery Canton was arrested, it was for drug possession with intent to sell. Unfortunately, what little evidence they had disappeared, which is why he was eventually released. Canton insisted he was wrongfully accused, but a substantial amount of heroin disappeared." Jenny cleared her throat, and it sounded like she took a drink. "Apparently, there have been some pretty heavy turf wars, and those drugs were a part of it. When they disappeared, things became unsettled. Both sides of that war believe Jeffery is the one who stole and hid the drugs."

Erica glanced at her son, who was playing a video game. Mac had a set of headphones that he'd allowed Peter to borrow. At the time, it was to keep noise down so people could nap. Now, though, she was thankful that he was unable to hear their conversation. "How do they know about Peter? Jeffery hasn't even seen him before. I seriously doubt he has newspaper clippings hanging on the wall."

"We may never know the answer to that," Mac said, his voice kind.

"Is Jeffery still missing?" The question came from Cole. "I wonder if they're hoping to use Peter to lure him out and then coerce him into giving back the drugs."

"That's the running theory right now," Jenny said. "I spoke with the hospital, and Juan finally regained consciousness. Police were waiting there to interview him. At first, he refused to talk until the officer started dropping the names of Marshal Smith and Wallace Cash. Apparently, the fact that other members of the crew had been identified was enough to scare him. He admitted that they were working for someone but wouldn't say who. He did verify that they were trying to kidnap Peter for ransom."

"With that much money in play, they won't be backing down." Mac's voice was even.

"That's all I have for now. You guys keep lying low, and be careful. I'll be in touch when I know more."

"Thanks, Jenny," Erica managed, even though it felt as though her throat was closing in.

"You bet."

The call ended, and all Erica could do was stare at a spot on the table. It was all too much. How was she supposed to protect her son against this?

She was vaguely aware of someone speaking her name, but it didn't register until Cole took her hands and tugged her up to stand beside him. Then he guided her past Mac and just inside his hotel room.

"We're going to figure this out, and you'll be back in Destiny before you know it."

"What if we never catch these guys? What if they give up for now and go back to Houston? How am I ever supposed to relax? How am I supposed to let Peter out of my sight knowing they're still out there somewhere?" Her voice caught.

Cole put his hands on her arms and rubbed them gently. "Because we *will* catch these guys. Mac, Officer Durant, and countless others who are working this case. We're good at what we do."

A tear broke through her defenses and made its way down her cheek right past the cut.

Cole used a single finger to wipe the tear away and then cupped her face with both hands. "I promise I will do everything in my power to keep you and Peter safe."

She leaned in to his chest, and he wrapped his arms around her and held her close.

Chapter Nineteen

Erica had a difficult time relaxing after the phone call with Officer Durant. She was currently straightening everything in the hotel for a second time. Thankfully, Peter was somewhat unaware of what was going on. They ate dinner and then took turns playing tic-tac-toe and hangman on the pad of paper the hotel had provided. After everything her poor boy had been through, he was asleep by nine.

Since they weren't sure how long they might be at the hotel, the adults took turns taking lightning-fast showers. It was after eleven, and Mac had just offered to take the first shift and keep an eye out, when his phone rang.

"It's Asher." He motioned for Cole and Erica to follow him into the adjoining room so they wouldn't wake up Peter. He put the call on speaker. "Hey, man. What's going on?"

"Listen, I've been thinking about the chain of events yesterday, and something didn't quite add up. Cole, you're one of the most observant people I know. There's no way these people trailed you all day, and you didn't notice. And

I certainly can't imagine them driving up and down the streets of Fredericksburg hoping to randomly run into your vehicle. Besides, a white truck in Texas? They're a dime a dozen." Asher paused. "I think they're tracking you somehow, and given how determined they are to get Peter, I doubt they just slapped a device on your truck."

Erica's stomach clenched as any relief she'd experienced in the safety of the hotel shattered.

Cole frowned. "You think it's on one of us."

The realization made Erica feel as though everything she wore or carried was contaminated. Her mind raced. "It had to have been when they were in the B&B while we were at football practice. But what would they have put the tracker on? Most of what we had with us yesterday was with us then, too."

"I don't know," Cole admitted. "On clothing or embedded in a pair of shoes. If they put it on something at the B&B that day, it could even be on something *I* own." He paused as though he'd thought of something.

"What is it?" she asked.

Cole strode over and snatched Peter's backpack off the end of the bed. "He didn't take this to the football practice on Thursday, did he?"

"No, he didn't. It's about the only time I won't let him take it along. I'd just end up holding onto it while he's on the field." Erica paused as a realization hit. "It was still at the B&B that night. You think the tracker is in there."

"I might be wrong," Cole pulled out a flashlight and began to rummage around in the different pockets and compartments. Less than a minute later, he pulled out a white, flat disc a little bigger than a quarter. He lifted it triumphantly. "And there we are."

"Yep, we found it, Asher," Mac announced.

"Okay, good. Slide it open and remove the battery. That will disable the tracking device," Asher instructed over the phone.

Cole quickly complied. "Done." He handed both pieces to Mac.

Erica was amazed that something so small could cause so much trouble for them. "Is there any way to find out who owns it or who's keeping track of it?"

"Not easily, no." The clickity clack of fingers on a keyboard could be heard in the background of Asher's call. "They all have a serial number which has to be registered to an account. There's a place online to add contact information in case the device is ever lost, but it's highly unlikely they would have left a calling card like that. Now, you can take it to the police, and they can get a warrant, and then insist on having the name and address of the person who had registered it. But that'll take time."

Cole rifled through his own backpack just in case, and Erica decided to do the same with her purse. Thankfully, she didn't find anything. She suddenly sobered as a thought sent a shiver down her spine. "If they've been tracking us all this time, then they know exactly where we are right now," she said in a quiet tone.

Mac nodded grimly.

Erica raked the fingers of one hand through her hair and gathered it into a ponytail at the base of her neck. "So why didn't they come after us again last night?"

"They had to regroup," Cole said. "Maybe they're waiting for someone to drive in to replace the guy I shot? Then it was daylight, and they couldn't just storm the hotel room with so many people coming and going."

A car door slammed shut outside, immediately silencing

all conversation in the room. They listened and heard another one.

Erica watched as Cole and Mac silently strode to the window. Carefully, they peered from the side where the curtain brushed against the wall so that no one outside could see movement.

Cole came back, his face dark with unease. "There's an SUV parked in the street behind the cars in front of the hotel room. It looks like two or three people are getting out. We can't fight them here. It's too risky when we don't know how many people there actually are."

"They're probably afraid that we're going to make a run for it now that the tracker has been shut off." Mac pointed to Erica. "Grab Peter and get to the next room now," Mac instructed. "Asher, call the police and let them know what's going on. I've got to go. We'll call you on the other side." He grasped his own bag and slung it over his shoulder before dialing a number on his phone.

Fear stabbed at Erica as she woke Peter up. Then she shoved her feet into her shoes and grabbed her purse.

Cole snatched his backpack as well as Peter's and reached for the boy who was stumbling out of bed. "Come on, big guy. Everything's going to be okay."

Once in Mac's room, he handed Peter his shoes and backpack. Then he and Mac locked the door between the rooms and barricaded it with a small dresser.

Erica helped Peter get his shoes on and then put an arm around his shoulders. Mac stepped in front of them. "When they break into the other hotel room, we're going to go out this door and around to my car on the other side. Cole is going to lead the way." He pointed to Peter. "You hold your mom's hand and don't let go. Erica, I want your hand on Cole's back so that he knows you're behind him. Do not make a sound, and do not look back. I'll be bringing up the rear to make sure no one is following us."

"Got it." She swallowed hard, reached for Peter's hand, and began to pray in a fervent whisper, "Father God, please put a hedge of protection around us. Help us get out of this safely."

"Amen," both men echoed in a whisper.

She looked for Cole and found him at the window, carefully peering around the edge of the curtains. Mac tapped him on the shoulder. "I've got this."

With a nod, Cole went to stand with Erica and Peter and guided them to wait closer to the door.

"Looks like two men," Mac reported. "They're going right for that door now."

Cole gave Erica's hand a quick squeeze before letting go again. "Be ready," he whispered.

Erica touched his back and tightened her hold on Peter's uninjured hand.

"They're going in," Mac whispered loudly. "Go. Now."

Silently, Cole opened the door and headed through it. He didn't hesitate as he turned right and rushed down the walkway in front of other hotel rooms. Erica had to jog to keep up, and she prayed none of them would stumble in the dim lighting. She could barely hear Mac's footsteps behind them.

Sirens sounded in the distance, and Erica's heart caught in her throat. If they got here in time, maybe this could all be over tonight. She prayed that would be the case.

They rounded the corner and reached the back parking lot. Cole ran to a small car closest to them and reached it just as the locks disengaged. "Everyone, get in quickly."

Erica broke away from Cole and led Peter to one of the

back doors. Her hand had just touched the handle when a scratchy voice bellowed from behind her.

"That's far enough."

She whirled to find the silhouette of a man on the sidewalk they'd just left behind. She couldn't see his face, but she recognized the voice. Marshal Smith.

He stepped out of the shadows, revealing a gun in his hand.

The sirens grew louder. They'd be here any minute. Unfortunately, they would be up front where their hotel room was. How long would it take for them to check back here?

"I had a feeling you might try to sneak out. I've had enough of these games. Give me the boy, or I'll kill you and take him anyway."

"No." Without hesitation, Erica guided Peter behind her and prayed that her body would shield him completely.

"Works for me." Marshal leveled his gun at Erica.

Cole came out of nowhere and stepped in front of her. At the same moment, a gunshot rang through the air, quickly followed by two more.

Erica flinched and closed her eyes for one heartbeat. Two. She expected to feel the hot metal of a bullet pierce her skin. When it didn't happen, she opened her eyes again.

Her gaze went to Marshal's limp form on the sidewalk. Mac kicked the man's gun away and bent to feel for a pulse. "He's gone." He holstered his own gun.

A rush of intense relief nearly made Erica's knees buckle.

Cole, who had shifted to one side of Erica, turned and cupped her shoulder. "Are you and Peter okay?"

Peter threw his arms around her. "I'm okay," he said, his words muffled.

"We're fine." A relieved sob traveled up Erica's throat.

Cole squeezed her shoulder before slumping against the car.

"Cole?" She reached for him as he collapsed on the ground. "No, no, no! Mac! I think Cole was hit."

That first gunshot. Cole had stepped in front of the shot that was meant for her.

Mac took a flashlight from his pocket and turned it on, illuminating a maroon stain on the front of Cole's left shoulder, and it was visibly getting bigger. Mac shrugged out of his shirt and pressed it against the wound. "Erica, hold this here. Push hard. I'm going to call for help."

Erica knelt on the ground beside Cole and placed her hands on the shirt.

"Mom?" Peter's shaky voice came from behind her. "Will Mr. Shepherd be okay?"

Hot tears stung Erica's eyes. "The doctors will be here soon, honey. He's going to be fine." *Please, God. He has to be fine.*

Chapter Twenty

Confusion. At first, Cole thought he was back in the hotel, asleep on one of the beds. Then a white-hot pain spread across his shoulder. He tried to take a deep breath, but the pain seemed to radiate into his chest. He put his hand against the source and groaned.

"Cole? Can you hear me?"

He did his best to force his eyes open. The bright light overhead made it difficult to focus on the face in front of him. "Mac?" He blinked to clear his eyes, finally seeing his half-brother's features more clearly. "What happened?"

Mac released a lungful of air. "Man, you had us scared. You're at the hospital. You took a bullet outside of the hotel. Do you remember that?"

Cole desperately tried to clear the cobwebs in his head. Slowly, the events of the night unfolded in his memory. He remembered leading Erica and Peter to the car. They were getting in when... He started to sit up, but the pain in his shoulder prevented it. "Erica. Are she and Peter okay?"

"They're fine. You're a hero, brother. You saved Erica's

life when you took that bullet." Mac put a hand on his uninjured shoulder. "And you need to stop trying to sit up."

"You're good?"

"Yes, I'm okay. The police apprehended the guys who broke into the hotel as well as the driver in the SUV. Marshal was dead on the scene."

Cole remembered seeing Mac spin around, his handgun at the ready. He gave a satisfied nod. "Nice shot."

"Shots. I actually got him twice."

Cole started to chuckle, then groaned again when it became too painful. "Remind me not to do that."

"I'm going to go get a doctor. Rest, and I'll be right back." Mac hesitated. "I'm proud of you."

Mac's words settled over Cole's heart as sleep claimed him again.

The next time Cole woke up, he was surrounded by the voices of the Durham family. He kept his eyes closed and soaked in the collective sound as they talked amongst themselves in quiet tones. "If you don't speak up, I won't be able to eavesdrop," Cole said.

He spent the next twenty minutes accepting hugs and assuring everyone that he was going to be okay.

Mac helped raise the hospital bed so Cole was partially sitting up. "There. I bet that's better."

"Much." He glanced around the room at the faces of Greg, Ruth, and Mac by his sides. Gavin, Lucas, Asher, and Livi stood at the foot of his bed. Relief and concern were written all over their features. "Guys, I'm okay. Truly."

Greg reached over and mussed his hair. "You're too stubborn not to be."

Laughter filled the room.

"You're not wrong." He scanned the room again and focused on Mac. "Where's Erica?"

"Her brother drove into town to bring her and Peter some fresh clothes. I think they went to meet him and get cleaned up. She hasn't left the waiting room since they brought you in." Mac gave him a knowing look.

Cole was disappointed that he'd missed them. He desperately needed to see that she was truly okay. "Will you please bring her in when she comes back?"

"I'll make sure of it."

Suddenly, everyone was asking questions at the same time.

Greg held up a hand to silence them all. Finally, he turned to look at Cole with that firm expression that usually meant he was about to reprimand someone. "What's this I hear about you wanting to leave the business? If that's true, you could have just told me. Getting yourself shot for some time off was a bit dramatic." The frown on his face gave way to his teasing smile.

Cole laughed and immediately regretted it. "Ohhhh. They did not give me enough morphine for this." He clenched his fist and breathed through the pain, but even that couldn't stop the smile on his face as he looked around the room.

Every member of the Durham family—his family—was there. For him.

"I'm not going to lie. I seriously considered leaving. But this mess right here is exactly where I'm meant to be. It'll take more than getting shot to get rid of me."

He soaked in the conversations as Gavin teased him about being a human shield, Livi made sure he was warm enough, and Asher assured him the business wouldn't have been the same without him. Ruth kept reaching over and lovingly running a hand over the top of his head. It wasn't long, however, before the pain and exhaustion threatened to take over, and his eyelids grew heavy.

"All right, everyone," Greg spoke up in his booming voice. The room fell silent immediately. "I think we've done enough damage here for now. Let's give Cole a chance to rest."

The family filed past, each one giving him a hug or a hearty handshake until Greg and Ruth were the only people left. They'd turned to leave when Cole called out, "Hey, can I talk to you two for a minute?"

"Of course, son."

It wasn't the first time Greg had called him that, but it was the first time Cole really took it to heart. He swallowed past the lump in his throat. "I wanted to apologize for all the headaches I caused you guys through the years. I was messed up. Still am, if I'm being honest. I gave you both a lot of grief and trouble. You could have tossed me out, and I wouldn't have blamed you. But you didn't." He searched for the right words. "Thank you for taking an angry kid who had no one and making me a part of your family."

There was no missing the tears in Ruth's eyes, and even Greg's were suspiciously shiny.

Ruth leaned in, carefully gave him a hug, then patted him lightly on the chest. "You were a challenging kid at times, but make no mistake: You were always worth it."

Greg nodded his agreement. "This family wouldn't be the same without you."

Cole drew in a steady breath and swiped a tear out of the corner of his eye with a knuckle. "Look, I know this is long overdue." Nerves flared, and he took a moment to steady them. "I'd like to call you Mom and Dad if that's okay."

"I'd like nothing better, son." Dad leaned down and rested his head against Cole's.

Ruth bobbed her head, tears freely flowing down her cheeks. "I'd love that."

They spent a few more minutes together before Cole was almost too tired to stay awake. As silence filled the room and his eyes closed of their own accord, he fell asleep with a smile on his face.

"Uncle Bryce!" Peter launched himself at his uncle. "Boy I'm glad to see you!"

"I'm glad to see you, too, kiddo." Bryce hugged his nephew and ruffled his hair. "It sounds like you took great care of your mom. I'm proud of you."

Peter stood taller as he cut a glance toward Erica. "I think we took care of each other."

"That's even better." Bryce handed him a backpack. "I've got some of your clothes and books in there."

Erica smiled as Peter dug through the backpack and pulled a book out. She turned her attention to Bryce. She stepped into his arms and welcomed his tight hug. "Thank you, little brother."

"You're welcome. I brought you fresh clothes too. Don't worry. Megan picked them out." He stepped back and winked.

"That's probably a good thing." She watched as Peter started to read a book about dragons for the fourth or fifth time. She hoped to have him take a shower before heading back to the hospital but decided clean clothes would be good enough.

On the other hand, a shower for herself was a necessity.

Bryce set the other backpack he'd brought in down on the bed. "How's Cole doing?"

Erica moved to the other side of the room and motioned for him to follow. "The doctors are saying he'll make a full recovery, although he may need some physical therapy to help his shoulder heal." She lowered her voice. "When he stepped in front of us and took that bullet..."

The chain of events flooded her mind and brought tears to her eyes. It'd happened so fast. Yet, every time she closed her eyes, it played out for her again in slow motion. "It was horrible."

He put an arm around her and gave her another hug. "I can imagine. I'm sorry that you went through that, but I sure am thankful that Cole was there through all of it. Have you had a chance to talk to him yet?"

"No. They were only letting family in, a person or two at a time, and he was sleeping. As soon as I catch a shower, we're going to head back. I got a text from Mac—that's his half-brother—that he was awake." Nerves twisted her stomach into knots. How could she possibly express how thankful she was to him for saving her life?

Bryce was watching her, a thoughtful look on his face. "Is he planning to come back to Destiny?"

She shrugged. "I don't know."

"He's a good guy. There's obviously a connection between you two. You owe it to yourself to give that a chance." Before she could object, he held up a hand to stop her. "Cole isn't Jeffery."

"No. He's not." If only she knew what the future held. In some ways, though, maybe it didn't matter. She'd already fallen for the man who had set everything aside to protect her and Peter.

Bryce wrinkled his nose and gave an exaggerated sniff.

"Why don't you get that shower, and I'll hang out with my nephew? Then I'm going to head back and check on Megan. She's still tired, and I hate to stay away for too long."

Erica smacked him on the arm. "I'm not that bad. But I will take you up on your offer. Thanks again, little brother."

"Anytime."

Twenty minutes later, Erica felt like a new woman. After a nice, hot shower and putting on her own clothes, she was ready to head back to the hospital. They'd said goodbye to Bryce, and she was just about to call Peter to make sure he had his shoes on when her cell phone rang. It was a Destiny area code.

"Hello?"

"Hey, Erica. It's Jenny. How are you doing?"

"I'm better. Peter and I are going back to the hospital to see Cole. He's finally awake and ready for visitors." Her stomach clenched with nerves. As much as she wanted to see him, she wasn't sure what to expect.

"I won't keep you long. I just got some information that I wanted to pass along. But first, please make sure Peter can't hear my side of the conversation."

Erica's brows rose. "No, he can't hear you at all."

"One of the officers I was talking to in Houston called me today. Jeffery Canton was found dead two hours ago."

Jeffery was dead? Erica wasn't sure how she was supposed to feel. "What happened?"

"They don't know. His body was found in a dumpster downtown. Most likely, he was killed over the missing drugs. Maybe the drugs were found, maybe Jeffery never stole them in the first place, or maybe his secret died with him. It's a mystery. But I figured you'd want to know."

"I appreciate it, Jenny."

"No problem. Are you sure you're okay?"

"Yeah. I mean, I'm shocked. A little sad—mostly because it's such a shame that he chose that life over his family." Erica looked to make sure Peter was still in the other room and lowered her voice. "And I'm sad for Peter. Someday, when he's older, I'll have to explain all of this to him. I just hope he understands that it has nothing to do with him and everything to do with a man who was broken and unable to change."

"Well, that boy of yours has an amazing support system in place. He'll be okay. You all will."

"Thank you."

"Now get back down to that hospital. And tell Cole I said hello, and that I'm praying for his recovery."

"I will. Thanks again, Jenny."

Erica hung up the phone with a heavy sigh. Jenny was right. Peter had so many people who were there for him and loved him. He was going to be just fine.

Twenty minutes later, they walked into the waiting room to find the entire Durham family there.

She'd met them all before because Mac had been kind enough to introduce her. Still, there were so many of them that it was a bit overwhelming.

Thankfully, Mac intercepted her with an understanding smile. "Cole was asking for you earlier. He might still be asleep, but I doubt it'll be for much longer. If you'd like to sit with him, I'll be more than happy to watch Peter for a while."

Erica looked down at her son, who nodded at her. "I guess that'll be okay if you're sure you don't mind."

"Not a bit. We've got this. Cole's in room fifteen. Just down the hall on the right."

Erica waited long enough to listen as Peter told Mac all about the new video game preview he saw. She smiled.

It faded, though, as she walked down the hallway toward Cole's room. Mac had said he was asking for her, so that was a good sign. Still, she couldn't help but be nervous. There was something between them, of that she had no doubt. But what if, now that she and Peter were safe, he'd made the decision to leave the family business and not move to Destiny? She certainly couldn't blame him.

She stopped outside of his room, closed her eyes, and took in a steadying breath. "Thank you, God, for bringing us through everything this last week. Help us know where to go from here."

Finally, she pulled the door open and stepped inside. The light was dimmer than it was in the hallway, and it took a moment or two for her eyes to adjust.

Cole was lying on the hospital bed, his eyes closed. His chest rose and fell with each breath. The white bandage on his left shoulder snagged her attention as she drew closer. She carefully reached out and touched the edge of it. The last time she saw him, she'd been trying to keep enough pressure on that very shoulder to keep him from bleeding too much.

He'd taken a bullet for her, and it could have killed him.

Tears filled her eyes and threatened to spill over when his hand moved.

He lifted it to cover her own. "Hey, you."

She shifted her gaze to his face, happy to see his brown eyes watching her.

"Hey yourself," she said, her voice quiet. "It's good to see you awake." Her voice cracked as an image of him lying on the ground, blood soaking his shirt, came to mind. She swallowed hard. "How are you feeling?"

"Better now." His voice sounded husky. "Thanks for coming. I needed to see for myself that you were okay."

"Thanks to you. Cole, you saved my life and Peter's, too. And all I could think about when they loaded you onto that ambulance is that I didn't know what I'd do if you died."

"But I didn't."

Suddenly cold, Erica crossed her arms in front of her and tried to push back the emotions that threatened to overwhelm her.

"Come here, sweetheart." He motioned her over and then shifted to his left to make room on the bed. "I don't know about you, but I desperately need a hug right now."

She nodded and then eased onto the bed next to him before resting her hand on his chest. She soaked in the warmth of his body and the comfort of his arm that held her close. They lay like that for several minutes before she spoke again. "I met your whole family. They seem really great."

"Yeah, they are." He pressed a kiss to her forehead. "I've decided I'm going to stay with Durham Security."

"Which means you'll be moving to Destiny?" She held her breath as she waited for his response.

"Yep." He lightly rubbed her arm with his fingertips. "I'd really like to get to know you better. Take you out on a proper date, preferably one where we aren't getting shot at."

Erica released a contented sigh. "I'd like that too."

"Good." He lightly kissed the tip of her nose and then her lips before resting his forehead against hers. "Because I can't imagine a future without you and Peter in it."

His dark eyes studied her, the emotion there confirming his every word. His heart raced beneath her palm, where it still rested on his chest.

She smiled and tilted her head for another kiss. "Neither can I."

Epilogue
Two Months Later

Erica looked at the for-sale sign in front of the B&B. The realtor had just added a "SOLD" sticker to the front, and suddenly everything seemed real. All their personal stuff had been moved out, and the new owners were anxious to take it over. Erica was glad that it would remain a B&B.

"You still okay with all of this?" Cole snaked an arm around her waist from behind and kissed her neck.

"It's scary, but I feel more relief than anything. I guess the biggest thing is that it's the end of an era, you know? There are a lot of memories tied up in that building. It's hard not to be a little sad."

She was excited about the future, though. She'd rented a small house not far from Bryce and Megan. It had two bedrooms, two bathrooms, and a nice backyard. Most importantly, the owners said it was okay for them to get a dog. She hadn't told Peter yet, though. She was hoping to surprise him for his birthday next month.

"How's everything going for you guys? Moving a household has been a challenge. I can't imagine trying to move a whole business."

Cole kissed her neck again and stepped back. He reached out and wrapped a section of her hair around one of his fingers. "Mom is an organizational genius. And Dad? Well, he was smart enough to hire people to do most of the heavy lifting. I think the biggest challenge is getting the new place ready to move in."

It'd taken longer than originally planned for some of the updates to be finished. Erica had seen pictures of the progress and couldn't wait to get a tour of the place when it was ready. It was going to be an impressive building for Durham Security Solutions to work out of.

"I'm looking forward to being here permanently. None of this traveling back and forth to visit when I have a day off." He reached for her left hand and ran his thumb over the engagement ring nestled on her ring finger. "It'll be nice to see you every day. And even nicer to never have to say goodbye once we're married."

"I can't wait." Erica placed her other hand on the front of his left shoulder. He'd made a full recovery after the gunshot wound but still experienced pain from time to time. She prayed that it would fade completely one day. "We've made it this long. I think we'll survive another nine days until you move here and another two months until the wedding."

"If you say so," he murmured as he drew her in for a long, thorough kiss.

Erica melted in the arms of the man she couldn't wait to spend the rest of her life with.

Special Thanks

Elizabeth, all of our brainstorming sessions and sprints were not only a huge help while writing this book, but they also made it so much more fun. I am thankful for you, my friend!

Denny, you are amazing. Your encouragement and friendship mean the world to me.

To the amazing members of my Readers with Heart team: I appreciate each and every one of you. Thanks for all you do.

Doug, thank you for always being there for me. You are my best friend, and I couldn't do this writing gig without you!

Heavenly Father, thank You for Your unfailing love and for always holding me close during life's storms.

About the Author

Melanie D. Snitker is a *USA Today* bestselling author who writes inspirational romance and romantic suspense. She and her husband live in Texas with their two children. They share their home with three dogs and two terrariums filled with small critters. In her spare time, Melanie enjoys photography, reading, training her dog, playing computer games, and hanging out with family and friends.

https://www.melaniedsnitker.com/

Books by Melanie D. Snitker

Danger in Destiny

Out of the Ashes

Frozen in Jeopardy

Beneath the Surface

Caught in the Crosshairs

Running from the Past

In Search of the Truth

Assigned to Protect

Brides of Clearwater

Marrying Mandy

Marrying Raven

Marrying Chrissy

Marrying Bonnie

Marrying Emma

Marrying Noel

Love's Compass Complete Series

Finding Peace

Finding Hope

Finding Courage

Finding Faith

Finding Joy

Finding Grace

Books by Melanie D. Snitker

<u>Love Unexpected Complete Series</u>

Safe In His Arms

Someone to Trust

Starting Anew

<u>Healing Hearts</u>

Calming the Storm

I Still Do

Don't Kiss Me Goodbye

<u>Sage Valley Ranch</u>

Charmed by the Daring Cowboy

<u>Welcome to Romance</u>

Fall Into Romance

A Merry Miracle in Romance